Hell
HOUSE

Dear Reader:

Reality shows have definitely become the craze on television. Collectively, tens of millions of people gather around their flat-screens, projector sets, iPads, etc. on any given day to live their lives vicariously through the drama, heartache and comedic moments of others. In Brenda Hampton's *Hell House*, we gain much insight into the inner workings of the minds of such contestants. Why would someone even agree to be on an elimination show? Live in a house with complete strangers for several weeks or months? Give up their connection to the outside world for an extended period of time? Put up with personal attacks on their character, or engage in mind games to seduce, trick, and break down other individuals? The obvious answers are money and fame but such is not always the most prominent reason.

In *Hell House*, Hampton introduces us to six unique, variously motivated people who quickly get out of control once they meet their new roommates. From the less-than-seasoned female contestant who struggles to pronounce big words but can work her way around a kitchen like no other, to a vain young man who is already wealthy but needed a break from his hectic lifestyle, readers are drawn into their intriguing mindsets from the very beginning. But this is only the first of three books. Like real elimination shows, people will have to vacate the premises one-by-one until a winner is declared. *Hell House* is a rare and bold concept that will surely garner much acclaim.

As always, thanks for supporting the authors of Strebor Books. We always try to bring you groundbreaking, innovative stories that will entertain and enlighten. For a list of complete titles, please visit www.zanestore.com and I can be located at www.facebook.com/AuthorZane or reached via email at Zane@eroticanoir.com.

Blessings,

Zane

Zane
Publisher
Strebor Books
www.simonandschuster.com

ZANE PRESENTS

Hell HOUSE

BRENDA HAMPTON

SBI
STREBOR BOOKS
NEW YORK LONDON TORONTO SYDNEY

Strebor Books
P.O. Box 6505
Largo, MD 20792
http://www.streborbooks.com

ISBN 978-1-59309-536-9
ISBN 978-1-4767-4617-3 (ebook)
LCCN 2013933668

First Strebor Books trade paperback edition October 2013

Cover design: www.mariondesigns.com
Cover photograph: © Keith Saunders/Marion Designs

10 9 8 7 6 5 4 3 2 1

Manufactured in the United States of America

For information regarding special discounts for bulk purchases, please contact Simon & Schuster Special Sales at 1-866-506-1949 or business@simonandschuster.com

The Simon & Schuster Speakers Bureau can bring authors to your live event. For more information or to book an event, contact the Simon & Schuster Speakers Bureau at 1-866-248-3049 or visit our website at www.simonspeakers.com.

Roc

I couldn't believe that I agreed to do this bullshit. And it surprised me when I stepped inside of the so-called Hell House in St. Louis and didn't see anyone. The *Miami Vice*-style glass doors left me with a dramatic first impression that was kind of dope. I could very well be satisfied living here for the next three months; the living conditions resembled a penthouse I used to have while selling cocaine. That was then, this is now. Now, I was on lock by my fiancée, Desa Rae Jenkins, who recently suggested that we needed to explore life and try different things. In other words, she was tired of my black ass hanging around her house and wanted a break from our relationship. I also needed a break, so I jumped on this opportunity to jet away for a while.

I dropped my Nike duffle bag at the door and glanced upwards at the vaulted, sloped ceiling. The smell of newness was in the air and the glossy marble floor in the foyer was polished to perfection, displaying a glare of my chocolate fineness. *Umph*, I thought while staring at the blurred image of me. I wet my thick lips, then headed toward the kitchen to scope the rest of the amenities in this immaculate one-story crib.

"What up? Anybody here?" I called out, cautiously taking slow steps down a narrow hallway that had framed pictures of modern art on the freshly painted white walls. My new Air Jordans left imprints in the cottony carpet that led to a spacious, sunken living room area on the right and an urban-style kitchen with stainless steel appliances to the left. Checking out my surroundings, I narrowed my eyes into the living room that was laid out with a horseshoe-shaped microfiber sofa and square pillows. A forty-two-inch flat-screen TV was mounted on the wall. Underneath the TV were bookshelves filled with many books for someone's reading pleasure—definitely not mine. Numerous multicolored beanbags were also in the living room, and I assumed they were there for chilling purposes.

The living room could be chalked up as simple, but the high-priced kitchen was kicking ass. Everything was white, navy or stainless steel. Navy pendant lights hung above a white rectangular countertop that was surrounded with wavy curved-back barstools that had a steel finish. The decorator damn sure needed a kiss, but she wouldn't get one from me since I was now a reformed man.

While thinking about Desa Rae, I eased my hands into my jean pockets and looked out a sliding glass door that viewed a backyard my hood relatives could only dream of. There was an Olympic-sized swimming pool with crystal-clear blue water, tennis and basketball courts, and rock waterfalls used for diving. The lawn was well manicured and lounge chairs were all over the patio. At 103 degrees outside, I damn sure knew where most of my time would be spent. Yeah, my skin color was already black as charcoal, so I wasn't worried about the sun baking it much more.

I was getting impatient and sighed after licking my lips again. The motherfuckers running this show told me to be here at two o'clock, but when I looked at my watch, it was already two-thirty. Deciding to see what else was up, I turned away from the kitchen to go check out where I would have to lay my head. I noticed that the carpet trail split into two directions, so I shifted to the left first, entering a modern bathroom with unique stainless steel faucets, a pearly white toilet and a shower squared with thick glass. All the white made me nervous. I sure as hell hoped that I wouldn't be shacked up in this crib with a bunch of nasty people. I was eager to see who those people would be, especially the women—for whatever reason that might be.

I backtracked to the other hallway and that was where I found a room with three full-sized beds against one wall and three beds against the wall in front of it. The beds were covered with multicolored comforters and colorful sheets. Wasn't feeling that shit and the beds were too small. Nametags with our names on them sat near the edge of each bed. One by one I checked out the names, noticing that the brothers were on one side of the room and the sisters were on the other. That didn't work for me either, so I rearranged some things. I put my nametag on the bed that was in between Chase's and Sylvia's beds. Jada's nametag I put between Prince's and Jaylin's beds. I hoped Jada wasn't the finest one in the bunch, but then again it didn't matter either way. I was on lock. That was today, didn't account for tomorrow.

There was no window in the cramped room, but there was one sizeable walk-in closet. It was obvious that all this room was good for was sleeping and fucking. Didn't think I'd be spending much time chilling in the bedroom, so I made my exit, realizing that time was moving on and my grand tour of this crib was over.

I took another look at my watch, then reached into my pocket to grab my cell phone. Somebody needed to tell me what the fuck was up. I was getting impatient. A nigga like me was beginning to think this was some kind of setup. I'd been in these situations before. My instincts were saying run! The information guide and itinerary that I received said the meet and greet of contestants would begin at two. It was way after two, so fuck it. I felt the need to jet, so I put my phone back into my pocket and grabbed my duffle bag. Once it was on my shoulder, I headed toward the door, but was stopped dead in my tracks when I saw a taxi pull up. I squinted as I peeked through the glass, trying to get a glimpse at the fine-ass woman whose peep-toe stilettos had touched the ground. She had long, light-skinned legs that were made for riding. I was eager to see her face, and as soon as she exited the taxi, I could feel my nature trying to rise. That ass was fat and those hips swayed with rhythm as she made her way up the long driveway. Her weaved-in ponytail swung from side to side and was tightly pulled back, making her hazel eyes slant. I sucked in a deep breath and backed away from the door. Checked myself again, while looking down at the floor and hoping that the white wife-beater I had on wasn't too laid-back. It showed my tats that so many women loved and I figured she wouldn't be able to look away from my bulging muscles. Lance Gross didn't have shit on me, but there were some who would beg to differ. This chick, however, was classy and I liked that. She wasn't *Full Figured* how I normally liked my women, but I could definitely work with her. Unfortunately, if this was Jada, I had already messed up by putting her nametag on the other side of the room. Big mistake, no doubt, but after this bullshit was over I was sure there would be plenty.

Chase

I saw his blackness through the door, but why wouldn't he come outside to help me with my bags? Some men were so lazy and he obviously wasn't the exception. I hoped that someone else was here to help me. I had about six bags in the taxi and needed some assistance. The taxi driver claimed that he had broken his leg, but my question to him was where were the crutches? He didn't have an answer for that and I didn't have an answer for my wallet somehow disappearing. That is what I planned to tell him, once I got my belongings out of his taxi.

Instead of pushing on the front door, I pursed my lips and knocked with an attitude. It was scorching hot outside, and I was dying for a glass of ice-cold water. But when the door flew open, my thirst was more than quenched by saliva that almost slipped from my wide mouth. The rule was to never let a man see me sweat, so I quickly clamped my mouth shut, trying to downplay my instant attraction to the brother on the other side of the door. With tattoos running up and down his arms, he looked to be straight out of prison. But so damn what! I loved a man who was a bit rough around the edges, and I'd had enough of the business-minded married ones with clingy wives who liked to start trouble. After seeing him, my whole attitude had changed. I almost broke a heel as I rushed inside to see if he had been invited to Hell House, too. Right now, it felt more like Heaven's House.

I held out my hand to shake his. "And you are?" I said, awaiting an answer.

"Yo baby daddy." He smiled, displaying those snow-white teeth against all that black. Lord have mercy on me. I couldn't help but to play along with him.

"Well, baby daddy, do you think you can help me with my bags? They're still out in the taxi. The driver claims that his leg is broken and he won't help me."

"I got you," he said, passing by me to go outside. His good-smelling cologne tickled my nose and left me standing in awe. I was in a daze until I heard his voice. It shook me from my thoughts.

"Wha...what did you say?" I said, watching as he walked back-ward down the driveway.

"I said, since I got you, you gotta have me, too. That's on a for real tip right there."

Okay, so his language wasn't all that great, but I still gave him a nod. If this worked out, yeah, I had his back, front, side and then some. I was single, loving it and hadn't made any commit-ments to anyone, especially since that trick, Liz, caught me in bed with her husband. Liz was my boss and that day still haunts me. I've been careful not to date married men with bright wives. If she wasn't bright then that was a different story. The hubby was considered fair game and nine times out of ten he was mine.

My baby daddy was trying to impress me by carrying all six bags into the house. A sheen of sweat covered his forehead and he pulled up his wife-beater to dab the sweat. I got a glimpse of his abs. The look of them almost sent me to my knees, begging him to slip something into my mouth. I wanted to rip his clothes off right then and there, but I didn't want to blow it, as I had done so many times in the past.

"Thank you so much, but please tell me your name," I said.

"Roc," he said. How fitting for a stallion of a man like him? "But before you tell me yo name, you'd better go outside to pay the taxi driver. He's about to clown on yo ass. I wouldn't want him to do that, especially since I'm enjoyin' the look of it."

I didn't respond, but since he was enjoying *it*, I made sure he got a good look at my butt as I sashayed back to the taxi. I could only imagine what Roc was thinking. My tight, gray skirt hugged my backside like a long lost best friend, and my red silk shirt was draped low in the front, showing off my 36 C's. I had no idea what I was going to embark upon coming to Hell House, but I was thankful that my attire was professional and sexy.

"How much do I owe you?" I inquired to the taxi driver while digging into my purse.

The Fred Sanford-looking black man cut his eyes at me and then he pointed to his meter. "The car was still runnin' while you were inside. You owe me a hundred and fifty-two dollars."

It sounded like he had gunpowder clogged in his throat. My hand quickly moved to my hip and the attitude was back.

"One hundred and fifty what?" I yelled. "Are you kidding me?"

He had the audacity to put up his hand, displaying the numbers. "Five. Two. Fifty-two and the meter is still runnin'."

"And I'm going to be running in a minute as well because that is too much money. Besides, I can't seem to find my wallet. Did I leave it on the backseat?"

Yep, he was playing me like a fool, but please *Don't Even Go There* because I could play him so much better. I opened the back door and bent over to feel the floor, as if I was searching for my wallet. Roc was getting a clear view of what to expect when he hit it from the back, and without any panties on, I bent further over.

"I don't know what happened to my wallet. Are you sure you didn't see it?" I said to the driver.

"No, I didn't see yo wallet, but you need to get my money or else there's about to be some trouble."

See, he just pissed me off. Some men hadn't a clue where to draw the line. Was he really going to beat my ass because I didn't have the money? No. I eased out of the backseat and closed the door.

"Unfortunately, I can't find my wallet," I said with a shrug. "Either you can call the police or overcharge some of your other customers to make up the difference."

"Or, I can get out of this taxi and fuck you up. That's what I'm about to do!"

He swung the door open and hopped out of the taxi like he was trained by Bruce Lee. Broken leg, my ass. I didn't have to say one word because my baby daddy was right there to intervene.

"What's up, old school?" Roc asked as he stood over the taxi driver in a very intimidating manner. "Why you out here tryin' to rip this woman off? You didn't even want to help her with her bags, and now you disrespectin' her over some money? She said she lost her wallet, so nothin' else needs to be said."

The taxi driver backed away from Roc, but I stood close behind him in case something popped off. If anyone was going to get cut, it wasn't going to be me. Baby daddy was going down by himself.

"Look, man, just get this broad to give me my money. After that I'm out of here. If not, I'm gon' have to call the police. If I have to go that route, things will get ugly."

Maybe so because baby daddy looked like the kind of brother who probably had warrants. I didn't want him to get arrested, so I tried to compromise with the foolish taxi driver by offering him twenty dollars. "Here," I said, handing the bill to him. "It's all I have. Take it or leave it."

He reached inside of the taxi for his phone. "Fuck this shit. I should've called the police from the get-go."

"Dialin' the police means some blood may have to be shed," Roc said. "So think before you act. I don't have any dollars on me right now, but give me yo address and I'll mail the rest to you later."

It was obvious that Roc was gangsta, but there was no need for blood to shed. The old man pondered what to do and then all of our eyes shifted to a triple-black Mercedes with tinted windows. We could barely see who was inside, but when the passenger-side door swung open, I staggered backward and almost fell on my ass. Baby daddy had a twisted look on his face and the taxi driver stared as if he wished he were a woman. Almost in slow motion, a light-skinned brother with dark shades shielding his eyes emerged from the car. The smell of money was blowing through the air and we all inhaled it. He knew he was the shit and the ones who never smiled always had a big ego. I surely wanted to ignore him, but couldn't. He threw up the deuces sign to the driver and the driver backed away to leave. Professionally dressed like I was, the tailored navy suit he wore couldn't be duplicated. It had to be made specifically for him and the way it clung to the frame of his body was breathtaking. From the tip of the natural curls in his hair, to those shiny, black shoes that hit the pavement as he swaggered forward, he was flawless.

"I hope I'm not too late," he said, looking directly at me behind his stare. He was still at a short distance, but I was speechless, until baby daddy cleared his throat.

"Too late for what?" Roc asked. "Ain't too much of nothin' happenin' yet."

Shiiiit, baby daddy needed to speak for himself. There were a whole lot of things happening—inside of my coochie, of course. I was too ashamed to elaborate.

As Mr. Handsome came closer, he moved like a theme of music played in his head. His eyes gave me an intense stare down, and when he pulled his shades away from his face, I felt like his addictive steel-gray eyes were firing bullets from an AK-47. His gaze was so powerful that it sent shockwaves throughout my entire body. Sadly, I could feel a slow drip of sweat sliding down my forehead. *Get it together, Chase, now! Never let a man see you sweat or else you're screwed!* Right about now, getting screwed wasn't a bad idea.

"Nothing happening," Mr. Sexy said to me, ignoring Roc altogether. They both were checking me out and that was a good thing. "If ain't nothing happening, why is everybody outside looking irate?"

The taxi driver couldn't wait to speak up. "I dropped her off at this house, and she left me out here, sittin' in the car for at least thirty minutes. When she came back, I told her that she had to pay up. She got mad, and the next thing I know, this man out here yellin' and threatenin' to hurt me for only doin' my job. I don't want no trouble from nobody, but this cheap bitch done tried to get over on me. If she don't pay up, I will call the police."

"First of all," Roc said, preparing his defense for me. "Get yo time straight because she wasn't inside for no thirty minutes. If you had not lied to her about your leg bein' broken, this wouldn't even be no problem. Fess up and admit to your laziness. I wouldn't pay you one damn dime either, so why don't you go ahead and call the police?"

I surely didn't want the cab driver to do that, only because the police might force me to pay the money. I hurried to speak up and was thrilled that Roc had already tried to make my case. "There's no need to call the police, but you need to cut what I owe you in half. Roc is right. I wasn't inside for thirty minutes and you're the one who is trying to get over."

The cab driver wasn't trying to hear what we were saying. He kept going on and on, and he even called me another bitch. I was about ready to let him have it, but then Mr. Handsome spoke up for me.

"Naw, she ain't no cheap bitch," the sexy man answered in my defense. "She too fine to fit into that category. But I agree— somebody definitely needs to pay you your money."

"That's all I'm sayin'," the taxi driver said, mean-mugging me.

Next thing I knew, Mr. Handsome reached into his pocket and pulled out a wad of cash that was barely secured with a diamond money holder. He flipped through three hundred dollars and gave it to the taxi driver.

"Problem solved," he replied to the driver. "Now jet before you catch a beat-down from this beautiful woman you done pissed off, or from thug lovin' who I know wouldn't mind putting his foot in your ass."

"All day, every day, especially when I feel a muthafucka is out of line," baby daddy shot back. But his comment was directed at the really cute one. All he did, though, was snicker and smooth walk his way toward the front door.

"Preciate you, bruh!" the driver shouted. "You are my kind of nigga!"

Mr. Sexy turned around, giving his head a slight tilt. He stroked his goatee and his eyes looked to be shooting real bullets at the driver who had obviously said the wrong thing. "My name is Jaylin Rogers. I don't go by no other name and calling me anything else will get you disrespected. You've been warned."

Well damn! I hoped he wouldn't be that upset when I referred to him as my baby daddy. At this point, I was confused about who I wanted to proudly wear that title. The driver threw his hand back and rushed back into the taxi. He sped off in a hurry. All I could think about was rewarding both of these handsome men for all that they'd done for me already. While observing Roc's backside as he walked in front of me, I was so sure I would be able to come up with something spectacular for my new room/playmates.

Jaylin

She was sexy and pretty—check. Nails done—check. Smelled good—check. Hair in order—check. Nice ass—check. No panty line—double check. Seems as if the only thing that concerned me was the status of her financial situation. I bet any amount of money that her credit score was fucked up. If she couldn't afford to pay the taxi driver, there wasn't no telling what else she couldn't afford.

In addition to that, the last thing I needed was to add another woman to my payroll. The ex-wife and ex-mistress were already milking me dry. Everybody had their hands out for something, and with all the cash I'd been dishing out, there was no way possible for me to retire again. I had to keep money flowing. As hard as I worked, there wasn't a chance in hell that I'd turn down a vacation or an opportunity like this one to get away. Three months sounded like a plan to me, but I had to check this place out to make sure I was down with it. If everything appeared to be in order, then I planned to call my best friend, Shane, and have him come back here to drop off my things. For now, though, my shit stayed in his car, until I felt comfortable with my surroundings.

For starters, the place was cool. It was nowhere near what I was used to, but what the hell? I liked white accessories, and from what I had seen about the house thus far, it looked spotless. I was digging the swimming pool, and when I stepped outside onto the patio, I noticed a nice-size workout area where I could exercise in the morning. There was also a game room with a pool table and bar. The bathroom, however, was a bit on the tiny side. As I looked at it, I realized how much I would probably miss my Jacuzzi. I closed the door and then made my way into what was supposed to be a bedroom. I was shocked to see how narrow and confined it was. It would take at least three of these beds to match mine, and what the fuck was up with the nametags and colorful décor covering the mattresses? I sat on one of the beds, making sure it was comfortable enough for me to sleep. It wasn't. I started to rethink the whole thing, but as I was in deep thought, I heard the door squeak open. In walked the woman who had snubbed the cab driver.

"Hello," she said with a bright smile. She took a seat on the bed in front of me, crossing her well-moisturized legs. "I see you checking out this house, huh? I am, too, but I wanted to thank you for paying the taxi driver for me. He was so rude to me; therefore, I felt no need to give him one dime."

I was trying to get a good read on this woman, so I didn't say much. I let her do most of the talking, yet kept my responses brief. "There's not much in here to check out, especially in this room."

She looked around, paying extra attention to the nametags. "So, whoever Jada is, she's supposed to sleep between you and Prince. As for me, my name is Chase and I'm to the left of Roc. He's the other nice-looking man out there, but I don't like to be the closest person to the door. Do you mind if I switch Jada's nametag with mine?"

I shrugged as if it didn't matter to me either way. It didn't. Chase switched the nametags and then she sat back on the bed directly across from me. She opened her legs wide, before crossing them again. My eyes shifted so quickly that I was sure she hadn't picked up on where they had flashed to. I saw her shaved pussy, and I hated for a woman to play games and tease me. Her actions reminded me too much of my children's mother, Scorpio. Strike one.

"So, you never told me," she said. "What do you think of this house? Can you see yourself staying here for three months with complete strangers?"

I sat back on my elbows and looked up at the cheap ceiling fan squeaking, as it turned in circles. "Maybe. Maybe not."

"What would be your reason for not staying?"

I shrugged. "Don't know yet."

"Are you always so short with people?"

She was irritating me. "Do you have a low credit score, and why are you asking me so many muthafucking questions?"

Chase's eyes looked as if they were going to tear away from their sockets. "My credit score is none of your business. I'm only trying to make conversation, but I get a feeling that you don't wish to be bothered. Whenever you feel up to a one-on-one, I'm sure you'll be able to find me."

She slightly cut her eyes at me and worked her hips from side to side, as she left the room. She was too sassy, too nosey, too broke, and something in her eyes said trouble. Strike three for her. I preferred to keep my distance.

I stood to stretch and massaged my forehead, trying to relieve the stress. My kids were on my mind, but I honestly needed a break from them as well. I would surely miss them, but it was a wise choice for me to see how everyone back at home would manage without me. With that in mind, I dialed Shane's number, but not before I switched Jada's and Chase's nametags. I hoped to have better luck with Jada.

"I knew you wouldn't be able to do it," Shane said, laughing. "You want me to come pick you up, right?"

"Nope. I want you to bring me my shit. Leave my luggage at the end of the driveway and I'll pick it up from there. I'll get disqualified from the competition if anyone I know is on the premises."

"No problem, but I can't even imagine what it is that you're about to do. I do not believe that you'll make it past one week."

I loved proving Shane wrong. "How much money you got?"

"Plenty."

"Yeah, thanks to me. Therefore, I bet you a quarter of a million dollars that I can and will stay here for the next three months. You down with that bet or not?"

"Three months? With no pussy? Hell, yeah, I'm down with it. More like three days, and best friend or not, I expect for you to pay up."

"Who says I will be without pussy? No matter what, though, my hand will work out just fine. Now, bring me my shit and I'll get at you in three months."

Shane laughed and hung up on me. He gave me the ammunition I needed to go through with this. From this moment on, I was down with whatever swung my way.

I left the bedroom, now looking at the brighter side of this. But as soon as I walked out, Chase was there to greet me.

"Here," she said, giving me a check. "I assume that your attitude stinks because you're out of three-hundred bucks for paying the taxi driver. I hate to do this, but I have a feeling that if I don't give your money back, you're going to make these three months miserable for me."

I took the check from her and looked at it. It was only for two hundred and fifty dollars; she had come up short. Trying to get over was the name of her game, but she had me fucked up. Her address showed that she lived in an area in St. Louis that I was very familiar with. I'll just say the area wasn't nothing to brag about.

"I can't accept a check that may bounce in my hand before it reaches the bank. This one has a negative balance, and because of your credibility, I have to reject it."

I ripped the check in several pieces and let the paper fall to the floor. Chase stood with her jaw dropped. "So, that's how you're doing it, huh? I mean, who are you? Where did you come from and how dare you talk to me like that?"

"If you don't like what I have to say, don't confront me with no bullshit again. Just because I paid the taxi driver, it doesn't mean that I took your side. Personally, I think you tried to fuck that man over, but that's just my opinion."

Chase folded her arms across her chest. Much attitude was on display and it was funny to watch her lose control like this. "I would tell you what you can do with your opinion, but you already know, don't you?"

I rubbed my goatee and licked across my lips. "No, I don't know. You seem like a woman who has no problem speaking her mind, so why don't you tell me?"

She threw her hands in the air. "You know what, forget it. I'm not going to waste my time with an arrogant fool like you, and as far as I'm concerned, the taxi incident is a done deal. If you were foolish enough to pay the taxi driver, that was your loss, not mine. I won't try to repay you again, and please don't ask me for your money back."

"I promise I won't. Now, are you done? Is it okay for me to get settled in, now that you got all of that off your chest?"

"If I had any say-so about it, you wouldn't even be allowed to come in here with that attitude. But since I don't, welcome, Mr.

Rogers. I hope you somehow manage to knock that chip off your shoulder and have a good time."

"I'm looking forward to it. Hope you are too."

As she choked on her next reply, I stepped around her and walked smoothly toward the door to catch Shane with my luggage. On my way there, I spotted Roc parlaying on the sectional couch with his feet propped on the table. His hands were behind his head and he was watching ESPN. Something about him irked me. Having his feet on the table, as if this were his damn house was tacky.

The overall objective to Hell House was to be the last one standing. I already knew I would be, but I had to skillfully plan this out and get to know how the others operated. Chase had already shown her weakness, so getting her out of here would be easy. It was time to see what was up with Roc.

I made my way down the steps and into the sunken living room. Roc saw me, but pretended as if he didn't. He kept his eyes focused on the TV, but I knew better. That was how I got down, especially when I wanted to make someone think they weren't important. Fucking with him, I reached for one of the magazines underneath his feet on the table.

"Do you mind moving your feet so I can get this?" I said.

Roc continued to look straight ahead. His feet did not move, but his mouth did. "Pull on it."

"Might rip it."

"Your problem, not mine."

"Wrong answer. It's gon' be your problem, if you don't lift your feet off the magazine I want to read."

Roc jumped to his feet and stood several inches away from me. His face was scrunched and madness was upon him. "What's up with you, *nigga*? And who the fuck you talkin' to like that? You need to holla at me like you got some sense. I ain't none of those good-old boys you be hangin' with at the country club, so watch yourself, potnah."

The ghetto made a lot of fools feel as if they were tough and invincible. Obviously, Roc was a product of that environment, but little did he know, so was I. This suit I had on was misleading, and when the time came for me to really get down with this idiot, I would have no problem doing it. For now, I had to accept the country-club membership that he had given me. But before I could say anything, Chase came into the room and stood next to Roc. She looked up at him.

"Chill, all right? He's not worth it, and the last thing I want is for you to get kicked out of here. I'm looking forward to having fun; fun that I thought you were interested in having. Right?"

Roc kept his eyes on me, but he backed up to the couch to sit down. Chase sat next to him, leaving very little breathing room in between them. I smiled to myself, knowing that pushing his buttons would be easy. Ole punk-ass nigga let a manipulative woman take his mind off the ass kicking I was *supposed* to get. That spoke volumes—he was weak.

I snatched the magazine off the table and glanced at the two of them cuddling on the couch. I cleared my throat to get their attention. "Listen. My bad for causing so much confusion, but I must confess that y'all make a real nice couple. Seem to have a lot in common and who knows? Things may work out for the two of you. Good luck with that sista, Roc. Chase seems like a real winner."

I winked and walked away.

"Hey, Jaylin," Chase said, halting my steps. I turned around, only to see her backside. She slapped her hand on her ass, shaking a chunk of it as she gripped it. "Kiss. My. Whole, entire ass, okay?"

For the first time, I smiled. "I would, but I can't get to it because your skirt is in the way."

To no surprise, Chase pulled up her skirt and I'll be damned if she didn't show her pretty ass. It was as pretty and round as I had imagined it to be. And anyone who knew me, they knew I was a man of my word and I loved to be *Naughty*. I walked over to her and bent down. Soaked my lips with my tongue and placed a delicate kiss on her right ass cheek. She blushed when I stood up, but I turned my attention to Roc, who sat on the couch with shock in his eyes.

"Get control of your girl," I said to him. "I think she likes me."

"Man, get on out of here with that shit. And like I said, that sounds like a problem for you, not me. Handle it."

No doubt, I would. I strutted away, but heard Chase say, "Screw you, Jaylin. You're not all that, you know?"

Yes, I was. And by now, she knew it.

My life had been going downhill since I let my ex-boyfriend, Kiley, get away. But I had to keep it moving. Therefore, when I was contacted about doing this challenge, I was all for it. I needed some excitement in my life. I got tired of sitting around all day arguing with folks on the phone over stupid stuff that didn't even matter. My girlfriends were all haters and all they wanted to do was go to the casino, get wasted at the clubs and eat. I was up to two hundred and thirty pounds now, but no one could deny how cute I was. Not even the man in my life. He wasn't about nothing but selling dope and trying to play hard. He somewhat reminded me of Kiley, but I was a fool if I ever thought I'd find a man to replace him. That man was so good to me and it was funny how I didn't realize all of that until after we had broken up.

My girlfriend, Portia, dropped me off in front of the Hell House, but it didn't look like a Hell House to me. I couldn't wait to get inside to see what was up, so I hurried to remove my bags from the trunk. Portia helped and then she gave me a hug.

"Be safe and write me if you can," she said. "You did say y'all can't have no phones, right?"

"That was one of the stupid rules, but I'mma do my best to keep mine on me. If I can't, then I'll write to let you know what's goin' on."

"You do that, boo, and don't hurt nobody up in there."

"I'll try not to, but you do know your friend."

We laughed.

Portia gave me another hug before she got into the car and drove off. I noticed several pieces of Kenneth Cole luggage at the end of the driveway, and I wondered whom they belonged to. Since I had two heavy bags full of stuff, I made my way up the long driveway and to the front door. By the time I got to it, I was out of breath. My jeans were so tight, they made my muffin top boil over my belt. My Black Girls Rock T-shirt was stretched across my 44 Double D's and the tennis shoes I wore had my toes crammed. It was so hot outside that my sandy-brown Afro was pulled away from my face, allowing the fullness of it to show. I never wore much makeup, only because my entire look was natural and I didn't need it.

I dropped my bags and reached out to knock on the door. What seemed to be seconds later, the door came open. Standing in the doorway was one of the most nice-looking brothers I had ever laid my eyes on. Actually, he was too cute and his cologne was intoxicating. Looked like he could easily be on the down low, and his tan had his body as caramelized as mine. I always made it my business to steer clear of men that I felt looked better than me and he did. His piercing gray eyes scanned me over, then he shot outside without saying one word.

"Excuse you," I said as he bumped my shoulder. "Damn."

I watched as he walked down the driveway to get his luggage. Making sure that he didn't bump me again, I picked up my bags and carried them into the house. It was beautiful inside, and I was in awe, thinking, *How Can I Be Down?* I kept it moving down the hallway and into a living room area where I saw a snooty-looking bitch sitting close to dark-and-damn-sure-lovely. Now, this dude was definitely my type, and my love for 50 Cent had finally come to an abrupt end. I didn't appreciate how close glamour girl was sitting next to him, so I played it cool.

"Hello," I said, sucking in my stomach and pulling down my shirt to make sure that it covered the wideness of my curvy hips. I was happy about my full figure, no doubt, but I wasn't sure if brotha-man appreciated healthy women. Maybe not, since the skinny woman next to him seemed to have his attention. So much so, that when I spoke, he only tossed his head back.

"Hi," the woman next to him said, wiggling her fingers and displaying a fake smile.

"Hello," I replied again, being fake as well. I dropped my bags on the floor and plopped down on the couch. It felt good to take a load off. "So, what's the deal here? Am I late?"

"No," the chick said. "We're still waiting to see what's up." She inched forward and extended her hand. "My name is Chase Jenkins. And you are?"

"I'm Jada Mahoney. It's a pleasant to meet you."

"Pleasure," Chase corrected me. "Not pleasant."

Oh, no, this bitch didn't go there. I realized that I was going to have to chop this heifer up like putting meat in a food processor. She smiled and sat back on the couch. All this fakeness was working me.

I looked up and saw Mr. Hollywood walk by with his luggage, but he didn't say a word to nobody. I wondered what was up with his attitude, but first I had to see what was up with all the dark chocolate sitting next to Chase. He was engrossed in the football game on TV, but I saw him checking me out from the corner of his eye.

"Who playin'?" I asked because I loved to watch football.

Unfortunately, Chase spoke up before he did. "The St. Louis Rams and the Cardinals."

"I was askin' him, though."

He stood and walked toward the kitchen area. "Roc," he said to me. "And she just told you who was playin'."

"Okay, Roc, but what the fuck is up with everybody's attitudes in here? Am I missin' somethin'?"

"Ain't nobody got no attitude, ma," Roc said, opening the refrigerator. He removed two bottled waters and tossed one to me. I caught it. "Just tryin' to check out the game. Handle yo business with yo bags and then come back to the livin' room so we can holla."

Now, he was singing my tune. I was grinning from ear-to-ear and thanked him for the water. Chase told me where I could find the bedroom, so I left to go put my bags in the closet they mentioned. When I opened the door to the bedroom, I couldn't believe my eyes. It was small, but was nice and comfy. I looked for my nametag, noticing that it was right beside Roc's. Chase's was on the other side of his. I figured the fine dude was inside of the walk-in closet because I heard him talking to someone on the phone.

"Because you be bullshitting, baby, that's why," he said to the person over the phone, as I went into the closet. "We'll deal with that when I come home. Until then, stay up and don't be over there crying because you miss me."

He put his phone in his pocket and then he shot a quick glance at me. I thought he was going to speak, but all he did was turn his back and hang more of his clothes.

The closet was humongous. Other luggage was inside, but no other pieces of clothing were hung. I had my stuff crammed into my bags. I decided to straighten my pieces now, so I didn't have to do it later.

"You almost knocked me down when you rushed outside," I

said, looking at the man's backside. Nice, but I was so sure another dude was getting it.

He turned around, scanning his eyes over me once again. His gaze was unnerving in a sense, but I looked at him in the same way.

"If an apology is what you're looking for," he replied nonchalantly. "You're not going to get one, especially since you were in the way."

My brows shot up so fast that my thick eyelashes were about to fall off. Was that his way of calling me fat? I was about to let this arrogant, curly topped-ass fool have it. Men like him made me sick and he needed to take his Harvard degree-carrying tail back to where he came from.

"An apology would be nice, but by the looks of your stuck-up gay ass, I'm sure I won't get it. The next time you bump me, though, expect some piano playin' and dirt layin' to go on. Somebody will be plannin' your funeral 'cause I'm not the one to mess with, just so you know."

He narrowed his eyes and he snickered a little, before turning back around. I wanted to punch him in his face; he was so irritating to me. I understood exactly what his look meant. All it said was I'm better than you and you ain't shit. Some black people killed me with that mess. Act like they ain't been through nothing and always looking down on other folks. By the time this Hell House mess was over with, he was going to learn to respect me. I would make sure of that.

I moved over to the side of the closet where he was to hang my things. His name-brand clothes were neatly hung and a few shirts were folded on top of the racks. I thought about what he did for a living. Probably sold drugs or had somebody selling for him. I wanted to ask, but a smart response could get spit in his face.

"You're either Prince or Jaylin," I assumed. "Probably Prince, since you're up in here actin' like the Almighty One."

"I'm whoever you want me to be. Gay, dead, a prince...take your pick."

"Ugh. How about an asshole then? Can you be one of those, especially since you're actin' like one?"

"I can do that, but first I may have to shove my dick in your mouth to silence that nonsense you're talking. Then, if I start calling you names that you're not going to like, your feelings gon' get hurt. Several words are on the tip of my tongue, so back the fuck up."

I tightened my fist, knowing that this fool was about to get it if he dissed me. Some men needed to be put in their place, and if I could handle Kiley, I definitely could handle him.

"Say it," I threatened, inching closer to him with gritted teeth. "I dare you."

The evil-looking bastard didn't appreciate my words or that I had moved closer to him. If I swung on him, there wasn't much room in the closet for me to get him good how I wanted to. So for now, I was thinking about scratching his face and poking those gray, disturbing eyes out with my fingers. He could tell that I was plotting to do something, so he backed up and shot me another stern gaze that was supposed to scare me.

"I don't know you, and I certainly don't know what the hell your problem is," he said. "But let me say this...you have crossed over into territory that you don't want to be in. If you want to keep getting at me like some kind of gangbanger, I will feel threatened. And if I feel threatened, that means, woman or not, you will find yourself knocked out cold on the fucking floor behind you. From this moment on, you need to think carefully about how you get at me."

He turned around and started straightening his things again. In no way did I view this fool as a man who would put his hands on a woman or hurt her. He looked too soft and his appearance showed that he was some kind of uppity nerd that would probably run home to tell his mama about me hurting his feelings. I was so annoyed by his sharp tone, by the way he kept looking at me, and because he had bumped my shoulder and still hadn't apologized for it. Not to mention that he had just threatened me. That was why I couldn't let this fool get away with what he'd done.

I tapped his shoulder to confront him again, and he swung around with madness visible in his eyes. Without any warning, he reached out his hand and gripped it around my neck. After that, several things happened and my entire body shut down. My breathing halted and my blood felt as if it had stopped flowing. I could not move, and I could barely see from the tears in my eyes clouding my vision. When I tried to turn my neck, he strengthened his grip and that was it for me. I felt hypnotized, and I was now in his command.

"Now that I have your attention," he said with a slow nod. "And I do have your attention, don't I?"

I followed suit and slowly nodded because he had added even more pressure to my neck when he squeezed tighter.

"Good. But now that I do have it, I want you to listen up and keep your big mouth shut. Can you do that for me?"

More pressure, so I slowly nodded again.

"I love progress, even when it has to be forced upon those who don't always know better. You do know better, don't you?"

I nodded again and all he did was smirk.

"I thought so, but in case you don't, I want to share a few things with you, just so we don't get off on the wrong foot while we're here. My name is Jaylin Rogers and you shall not refer to me as anything else. I'm a straight man, and I do not take bullshit from others too lightly. I will make yo ass pay for fucking with me, and if you feel as though you can't control yourself when you're around me, then I suggest that you keep distance between us. Because the next time you interrupt me with your bullshit, the punishment will be nothing like this. What I will do to you will hurt, and the last thing I want to do is go around hurting women. Maybe with my dick, but surely not with my hands."

At that moment, he snatched his hand back and it seemed that my whole body started functioning again. I could breathe, I could move my mouth and my blood was pumping. Iron Man turned back around, ignoring me again. I opened my mouth wide to suck in air I had lost, and I rubbed my neck, making sure it was still there. I didn't know if I had been unconscious or not, and it felt like he had done some type of voodoo shit on me. That was so messed up, but I had to let him know that his actions weren't cool. This time, I didn't tap his shoulder and I preferred to keep my distance.

"Uh, excuse me, but what in the hell did you just do to me? Please don't ever put your hands on me again, and if you think that a chokehold is going to silence me, you are sadly mistaken."

"I swear, some muthafucking hoes prefer to learn things the hard way," he said, shaking his head, but not turning around. When I looked up and saw another chick waiting to put her things in the closet, I stormed out of it. I was further away from him, so I felt safe talking back and responding to his hoe comment.

"Stupid bastard, the name is Jada!" I shouted from outside of the closet, per his request to keep distance between us. "Oooo, just wait! I got somethin' for that ass! You gon' be somewhere leakin', trust me!"

I marched out of the bedroom, thinking of ways to get him

back for what he'd done to me. I also wasn't sure if coming to this house was the right doggone decision, and the last thing I wanted to do was fistfight with men. That was something I'd done mostly all my life, and I was sick of it. Maybe my approach toward that idiot was wrong. I did want to start off on the right foot, but after what he'd done, I didn't know if that was possible.

Sylvia

I was skeptical about joining this challenge, but what did I have to lose? I'd been back in St. Louis for a little over a year now, trying to piece my life back together after falling in love with my best friend's husband, Jonathan. She thought I was being *SLICK*, but I wasn't. Jonathan and I worked together, and when I looked around, one thing just led to another. I still had deep feelings for him, but he recently told me that after his and Dana's divorce, that he was engaged to another woman. The news truly broke my heart and it felt shattered into a thousand pieces. At this point, I needed to get away to reevaluate where my life was headed from here.

I entered the Hell House on Sunday, September 16th, expecting for it to be a nightmare. But what I found was a handsome young man sitting next to whom I assumed to be his woman. They seemed nice and introduced themselves as Roc and Chase. The conversation was cordial and they directed me to take my luggage into the bedroom. That was what I did, but I halted my steps when I heard two people going at each other in a closet. I stood in the doorway, trying to put two and two together and remember where I had seen the man inside of the closet before.

"Don't I know you from somewhere?" I said, interrupting his harsh words to a chubby woman with fire in her eyes. She looked mad as hell and stormed out of the closet like a category 5 hurricane was upon her.

"Stupid bastard, the name is Jada!" she shouted. "Oooo, just wait! I got somethin' for that ass! You gon' be somewhere leakin', trust me!"

"I hope so and I'm looking forward to it, you non-talking—" He paused and glanced at me. "Know me from where?"

"I'm not sure. You look so familiar, but I can't put my finger on it. Anyway, I'm Sylvia."

"Jaylin," he answered, then placed his cologne on a shelf. "Not sure where I know you from either, but considering that I know a whole lot of women, ain't no telling. Just glad I switched those nametags again."

I didn't understand what he was saying about the nametags, so I didn't comment on that. "So, you've had that many women where you can't remember who you've met before, huh?"

I couldn't help but to laugh. This man was a knockout, and I was sure keeping up with his women was difficult. I knew he hadn't had me—not yet anyway.

"Women, knuckleheads, losers…whatever you want to call some of them. But as nice looking as you are, I would remember you."

I blushed, definitely appreciating the compliment. The thirty pounds I lost must have helped and the long braids I had done last weekend made me look younger. If I didn't do anything else, I took care of myself. My whole attitude was much better, and I realized that hurting other people to get what I wanted wasn't the best way to go. Losing Jonathan and my best friend, Dana, was a wake-up call.

"I appreciate the compliment, Jaylin, and I don't have to tell you how much I think you got it going on, do I?"

I swear his smile was to die for. He teased me and it was good to see that he had a great sense of humor. "Go ahead and tell me," he said, folding his arms across his chest. "Let me hear it, baby, and give it all you got."

I playfully pushed his shoulder, refusing to comment and let his head swell anymore. "Later," I said, walking giddily to the other side of the closet in my tight red pants and stilettos. I figured he was checking me out, and when I turned around he was.

"You ain't no fun, Miss Sylvia. And don't tell me you're too chicken to speak."

Disagreeing with what he'd said, I folded my arms and took a few steps forward. "I'm a lot of fun, just wait and see. But in the meantime, I need to hang up my clothes and think hard about where it is that I know you from."

"Let me know when you come up with something. I'm about to get out of here and go make some noise with the other people out there. See you when I see you."

Jaylin left the closet and all I could do was sigh from relief. He definitely made me feel some kind of way, and my thoughts hadn't turned this naughty in a very long time. I was even more hyped about being here now, thanks to him.

After I finished hanging my clothes and getting my accessories in order, I left the room to go join the others. Everyone was sitting in the living room area watching the football game. I sat next to Jaylin, since he was on the far side of the couch away from the others. He didn't take his eyes off the television, and neither did Roc who sat with his legs propped on the table. Jada was dipping her hands into some of the peanuts on the table and popping them into her mouth. And Chase kept eyeing Jada from the corner of her eye. I could tell they wouldn't get along in the house, and I didn't know if I would be able to cope with them either. Jada had already proven herself to be a nuisance and Chase was too catty.

"No offense," Chase said to Jada. "But I hope your hands are clean. Someone else may want some of those peanuts, so would it be asking too much if you went and got something from the kitchen to put your peanuts in?"

Jada stared at Chase with her jaw dropped. "While you're hopin' that my hands are clean, I'm hopin' that your ass is, since you got it all tooted in the air for others to see it. If you want me to find somethin' to put my peanuts in, why don't you get up yourself and go get it? If not, then shut the hell up and keep on watchin' TV. Thank you."

"Look, you don't have to get all snippy about it. I was merely making a suggestion, and with all of us being in this house, cleanliness is very important."

"You got that right," Jaylin said, adding his two cents. "I get what she's saying and nobody wants to dig their hands into a bowl of peanuts that you've, basically, washed your hands in."

Jada jumped up from the couch and snatched the bowl of peanuts from the table. "I see we got ourselves a set of house Negros in here. They want things sparklin' clean and they gots to make sure ain't no germs bein' spread 'cause Massa gon' come up in here and whip all our butts." She rolled her eyes and bolted out of the living room in a rant. "Give me a damn break. It couldn't be that serious."

In disbelief, all of our eyes shifted around the room. Jada took her ghetto self to the kitchen and dumped the bowl of peanuts in the trash. She opened the pantry, and a few seconds later, she pulled out a packet of Orville Redenbacher's Gourmet Popcorn and put it into the microwave. The sound distracted the men from watching the game and they both appeared very irritated. Jada, however, didn't care. Once she was done with the popcorn, she came back into the room, doing the Cha-Cha dance while throwing popcorn into her mouth. She plopped down on the couch and reached the bag out to Chase.

"I don't mind sharin'," Jada said. "Do you want some or do you think the kernels may do more damage to your rotten teeth? I thought I saw a little corruption goin' on in your mouth when you had it open."

This Jada chick was out of control and none of us could believe how bold her comments were. You would have thought that Chase cussed her out or something, but what Chase had asked for was simple, as well as necessary. I was staying out of this. By the looks of things, Chase could handle herself.

Chase opened her mouth wide. She pulled on the sides of it with her finger, so Jada could get a good view of what was inside.

"There's nothing rotten in there, sweetie. Don't know what you were looking at, but maybe you need to pull back on the popcorn and—"

Roc let out a deep sigh and silenced everybody—for at least a minute. "And maybe both of y'all need to chill the hell out so we can watch the game. Damn. Is it that serious?"

"Hey, that's what I want to know," Jada said, shaking her head from side to side. "All of this over some salty peanuts that tasted off brand. And this popcorn ain't hittin' on much either, but I'm still willin' to share."

She reached the bag out to Jaylin. He ignored Jada and that caused her to snicker.

At that moment, I felt very skeptical about this. Jada seemed a little off—kind of mentally challenged. Either that or she was a true attention seeker. That quickly became the case because she did not shut her mouth until a slender white man with blond hair entered the room and introduced himself as Jeff, the producer of *Hell House*. He apologized for interrupting the football game, but said that he was there to discuss a few things.

"I also want to give everyone a tour of the house and we do need to go over the rules."

We all listened in, as he stood in front of us dressed in khaki pants, a plain, button-down blue shirt that was neatly tucked into his pants and shiny loafers. His ocean-blue eyes were breathtaking, and his overall appearance showed that he was there to discuss business.

"First, let me say that I'm glad to see that most of you made it here. I thank you all for your willingness to do this challenge, but there are a few things that we need to go over before we get started. The rules are the most important and they must be followed. Not abiding by them can get you immediately kicked out of the house and no one wants that to happen. So for starters…no cell phones, no leaving the premises for three months, no outsiders allowed inside, no life-threatening violent behavior and no exceptions will be made for anyone. There will be a weekly schedule placed on the refrigerator for the person who has to cook and clean for the day. There are plenty of snacks, but if the person on the schedule doesn't cook, you don't eat. If you don't like what they cook, don't eat it. If they don't clean, the house stays messy. If you want to clean of your own free will, do it. No one is allowed to sleep in the living area or outside and you must sleep in the bedroom. There is one TV and one computer. Take votes on what to watch and minimize your time to one hour on the computer so others can use it. We've already installed cameras in each room, with the exception of the bathroom. If an emergency happens, you will have to stand in front of any camera to signal us or you can email me. We can be here in less than five minutes, but email may take longer. The cameras will roll twenty-four-seven and everything will be recorded."

Chase raised her hand. "Excuse me, Jeff, but I changed clothes in the bedroom earlier. Are you saying those cameras were record-ing me?"

"I'm not sure if the cameras were on then, but they are on now."

"What if I had a hole in my underwear that I didn't want anyone to see? There needs to be some kind of privacy in that room, don't you think?"

Jaylin responded before Jeff did. "You still have on the same skirt and lugging the same panty-less ass that you told me to kiss when you came through that door. Stop with the what-if questions and let the man get finished."

"Oops." Jada giggled and laughed out loudly. "That shit was direct and funny as hell, but he still needs to be put in his place."

Jada cut her eyes at Jaylin, and Chase shot Jada and Jaylin dirty looks. Chase knew darn well that she didn't have any holes in her underwear. All she was doing was trying to get some attention, like Jada. I could already tell that living here with these kinds of women wouldn't be good.

"You need to change clothes in the bathroom," Jeff said. "Are there anymore questions about what I said?"

This time Jada spoke up. "I got a couple of questions. One question is, are we allowed to knock the livin' daylights out of people who offend us? Two, are there any washin' machines around here? I didn't see any. And what about alcoholic beverages? Every now and then, I need a little somethin' strong to get my adreline goin'."

Didn't she mean adrenaline? I thought. I guess so when I saw Jaylin shake his head and Chase open her big mouth. She was rubbing me the wrong way already. I didn't like her.

"That's adrenaline, sweetie," Chase said with a little snap in her voice. "You really need to get it together."

Jada pointed to herself. "Are you talkin' to me, little girl? I'm goin' to pretend that you're not. That way I won't have to mop this floor with that damn wig you wearin'. I can already tell that it's not gon' work with me and some people in here. And if these so-called educated people know a little somethin', they best to leave me the hell alone. Okay, sweetie? Ugh, so damn irritatin' and what kind of woman calls another woman sweetie?"

"A woman who has no problem showing you some respect, but she will beat your ass if she has to. Now, cool out and watch who you're talking to. Please."

"Forget all the nonsense," Roc said, standing up and stretching. "Where did you say we can find the vodka and yack?"

"The what?" Jeff said with a confused look on his face.

"Cognac," Jaylin responded. "Top of the line, if you got it."

Him and Roc bumped fists and then Roc sat back down.

Jeff pointed toward the kitchen area. "Behind those double doors over there are a compact washer and dryer. Feel free to use them. Alcoholic beverages can be found behind the second set of cabinets over there, and outside at the bar in the game room. Have at it. As for physical confrontations, we are all adults here, and I recommend that everyone figure out a way to control themselves and get along with others. That's what this challenge is really about, so think about your actions before you do anything stupid. Now, are there anymore questions before we begin the tour?"

"Don't put shade on shit," a young man said as he stepped into the living room. "Tell me what the hell is in this for me?"

His hair was braided to the back and jeans were sagging so low that he had to hold them up. The oversized shirt was too big on him and a diamond necklace with the initials SS on it hung from his neck. I moved my purse closer to me and noticed that Chase and Jada had done the same. If he was going to be living inside of Hell House with us, God help us all.

Prince

I said it before and I'll say it again…I loved putting fear in the eyes of people who didn't know shit about me. They always judged a book by the cover and were never willing to look inside of a person to see what was really up. Yeah, I was catching some heat across town. That was why I chose to come to this place. Plus, there was a note that said money might be given to the winner who played by the rules. I needed some dollars, so I was down with the program. I was late, but I was here. Had to clear up some shit with the li'l mama in my life, Poetry Wright, just to make sure everything would be good between us if I was absent for three months. She said it would be, and I was happy about my girl being down for whatever.

All eyes were on me, but I was waiting for homeboy to answer my question. If money wasn't involved, I wasn't going to waste my time. Bills had to be paid, my Laundromat business was suffering and the only thing that was going strong was my liquor store. I was counting on that to pull me out of my personal recession, but if things didn't go well, I needed a backup plan. This was it.

"Prince," the white man said. "My name is Jeff. Have a seat and I'll be happy to tell you what else may be in this for you."

I walked over to the couch and sat next to the dark dude who I had seen a few times in the hood. I wasn't sure if he knew me or not, but he gave me a nod before I took a seat. The other wannabe pretty nigga didn't say nothing. I wasn't down with the way his uptight ass had looked at me, nor was I down with the hoes snuggling with their purses. Those bitches knew better. If I wanted their shit, I would take it.

"Pertaining to money," Jeff said, continuing on with his conversation. "The last person standing may be in a position to win one hundred thousand dollars. There are some stipulations, but—"

"One hundred thousand dollars!" the hefty chick shouted. "Canal Street in New York, here I come! I'mma get me an assistant Coach purse and some coochie glasses."

The other chick with a ponytail gave her a high-five. "I know that's right, but you know it's Gucci, right?" she said. "Time for a real Coach purse and a new car."

Obviously, these tricks didn't know what real money was. One hundred thousand dollars wasn't nothing to brag about, and since the pretty nigga didn't flinch, I could tell he wasn't moved either. Neither was the dark dude. Seeing him shaking and moving in the hood, I figured he probably made that kind of money in one week. But looking at it from another perspective, the money would come in handy. I was the real *Street Soldier* in the room, so I was sure that the money would fall into my pockets real soon.

"Stipulations that require everyone to follow the rules," Jeff said, looking at me. "I'll say it again…if you're caught disobeying the rules, we'll ask you to leave."

"Why the fuck you lookin' at me? I have no problem playin' by the rules, but I need to know what they are again. I guess I missed out by bein' late."

Jeff repeated the rules, and since they were cool with me, I stood up and followed along with everyone else as he gave us a tour. Before he started, he asked that we all introduce ourselves to each other. I told everybody that my real name was Jamal, but I preferred to be called Prince. After the introduction was over, the tour started in the foyer. Jeff pointed to a small sitting area that included a white leather sofa and a couple of chairs. Jada was the only person who had walked into the room to take a seat, even though Jeff said that he preferred we not utilize that particular room as much. She rubbed her hands on the leather, claiming that her friend had a sofa exactly like that one at her house.

"I mean, it's just like this. We picked it up at Big Lots about three weeks ago. That thing was real cheap, and I can understand why you said you didn't want nobody to come in here and sit. Cheap stuff never lasts for long, and I told her tail that when she bought it."

All of us just looked at each other, confused. This chick was weird as fuck, and when she referred to the rug on the floor as an organic rug, I almost lost it on this dumb broad. What school did she go to? Thank God that Jeff opened his mouth to address her ignorance before somebody else did.

"I can assure you that the sofa didn't come from Big Lots, and the rug is an Oriental Pakistan Ziegler rug that was hand knotted and—"

Jada cocked her head back and frowned. "Pakistan? So, you tellin' me Bin Laden could've made that rug before he was killed? Let me get out of here. I definitely don't want to be puttin' my feet on nothin' that fool made."

Jeff sighed a little and the rest of us remained in disbelief. Nobody told me I'd have to be living in this house with a mental patient, and unfortunately, her bullshit didn't stop there. While Jeff was showing us the elegant dining room, Jada had picked up a piece of china from the table and was glaring at her reflection. Using the china as a mirror, she was working her hair and shit, while sucking her teeth. You could always tell a bitch who wasn't used to nothing because they didn't know how to act. It was hard to concentrate on what Jeff was saying, when she was up in here acting like she had ADD.

"Shoot," she said, still sucking her teeth. "Is that a piece of meat in my teeth? Jaylin, come over here and look at this. Tell me if you see anything in between my teeth."

That nigga's face was flat, but he walked up to her with his hands in his pockets. The suit he had on was nice, and I don't ever think I had a suit in my possession that fit me like his did him. Either way, he squinted to look at Jada's teeth, while she kept them on display.

"I don't see no meat, but I do see a stick of butter. Be sure to take care of that when you get a chance."

The chicks to my right laughed, but Jada pursed her lips.

"Baby, you don't see no butter on these teeth, and Jeff got way more on his than I do."

Embarrassment washed across Jeff's face. He tried to play it off by laughing, though, but the man had had enough. Jada claimed she was only kidding, but she wasn't because his teeth could've used the attention of a dentist.

Jeff also told us to limit our time in the contemporary dining room, but I wasn't so sure about that. I definitely had to get my mind right because there was a time when I would've bagged up some of this shit and taken it to the pawnshop around the corner from my house. Everything on the table looked expensive and there was a possibility that I had hit the jackpot. Then again, the new me wouldn't even go there.

It took about thirty more minutes for us to tour the entire house because Jada and Jaylin kept throwing snide remarks and jabs at each other. I couldn't tell if they were playing or not, but the shit got on my nerves. Roc griped about the nonsense, too, but him and that Chase chick were very cozy with each other. While paying extra attention to my surroundings, I saw Roc taking peeks at her and Sylvia's asses. I had checked the women out too, and I had to admit that they had it going on. Jada also, but she was too damn silly. I couldn't imagine myself being with a chick with that much energy and playfulness.

Once the tour was done, I asked to be excused so I could go take a leak. Jeff said he didn't have much else to share, so I dropped my duffle bag and made my way down the hall. When I got there, I lowered the toilet seat and sat on it. Rolled up a fat-ass joint, then I lit it. My thoughts were on my headaches back at home. Seemed as if trouble had a way of following me. If I disappeared for a while, maybe things would chill. I suspected this place wouldn't be too bad. As long as I kept my distance from the others, things would be cool.

I filled my lungs with smoke from the joint and swallowed to get the real rush I needed. The weed was fire, and after several more hits, I was blazing. I looked around at the bathroom, wondering how in the hell all of us would be able to share it. I mean, the smell of my shit wasn't nothing to play with. Anybody entering the bathroom after me would definitely have something to deal with. I laughed from the thought. Leaned forward to rest my elbows on my knees and chuckled some more. But as I was about to take another hit from the joint, somebody knocked on the door.

"Speak!" I shouted.

"You almost done?" the voice said. I could tell it was the dark dude, so I put the joint out with the tip of my finger and placed it into my pocket.

"Hold up." I opened the cabinets and looked for some air freshener. I didn't want anyone to get a whiff of what I had been doing.

"Hurry up," he fussed. "I need to drain the big vein."

I quickly found the air freshener underneath the sink and sprayed it before waving my hands around and opening the door.

"Damn," the dude said as he came into the bathroom with his jeans already unzipped. "What took—" He paused to sniff the air. "Never mind. I already know what's up."

I wasn't trying to be caught up in the bathroom with this nigga, but I wanted to know if he had seen me around.

"Ay, don't you be hangin' out near St. Louis Avenue, Newstead and Natural Bridge?"

"Sometimes," he said with his dick hanging out of his jeans and peeing. He looked relieved. "I have an auto body slash mechanic shop off St. Louis Avenue named after me."

I thought about the area in my head and it hit me. "Roc? Are you Roc Dawson?"

"In the flesh."

Roc had a decent reputation in the hood and many people respected his hustle. He was definitely on the come up. "Well, I'm Prince. Heard a lot about you, and the word is, you good people."

"All good," Roc said, washing his hands and wiping them on a towel. "And St. Louis ain't as big as you think. Heard some things about you, too, Street Soldier."

I smiled at the thought of him even knowing me. Didn't matter if it was bad or good; I didn't give a fuck.

"So, what's been shakin' so far with this Hell House thing? I see that Grey Poupon-eatin' nigga out there lookin' like he got beef with some people. I hope not with you."

"I don't know what's up with that fool, but any man that angry ain't got nothin' but women problems. I'mma keep out of his way because I may have to shank him for steppin' to me the wrong way."

"Straight up?" I said with my back against the door. Roc seemed down-to-earth, but too bad I was going to have to snake his ass to win this money.

"Where the weed at?" he asked.

"What weed?"

"Fool, don't play. You got this bathroom lit up. That shit you got assaultin' my nostrils in a good way."

I hesitated, but pulled the blunt and lighter from my pocket, giving them to him. He lit the joint, inhaled the smoke and sat on the toilet.

"Ahh," he said. His eyes watered after the first hit and he damn near choked on the smoke. "Dis' shit is the truth! Where did you get it from?"

"I never reveal my sources, but if you ever need some more, come see me."

Roc nodded and continued to hit the joint. "So, what's the plan, Street Soldier? You know damn well that you ain't gon' be able to knock me out of this competition, right? We come from the same streets and we know how to play the game, instead of allowin' it to play us."

"I feel you on that, but I do intend to be the last man standin'. By any means necessary, you will have to go."

Roc laughed and gave the joint to me. "I like you, Prince, but this competition you will not win. You may as well pack it up and head back to your mama while you got a chance."

Roc left the bathroom, leaving my heart aching as I thought about mama. Why did she have to leave me like that? It was because of her that I'd had so many setbacks in my life, but I still loved her. I wanted the best for her, but I got tired of injecting myself into fights with her men. One day, somebody was going to get killed. All I could do was hope that when that day came, it wouldn't be me.

Roc

Jeff took our cell phones, jetted, and, now, Hell House was in full swing. Chase was in the bedroom hanging up her clothes, Sylvia was on the computer, and per the schedule it was Jada's turn to cook. She was in the kitchen whipping up a late dinner for us. She bitched about being the first one on the schedule, but in this crib, we didn't have many choices. If you didn't play by the rules you were ass out.

Jaylin, Prince and I were still in the living room watching football games, but none of us had said much to each other. I figured Jaylin was still *swoll* about the incident with Chase all over me, but I didn't give a damn about that freak. I wasn't the type of brotha to beef with no nigga over a broad like her, especially if her name wasn't Desa Rae. I was already missing my baby, even though she had some funny-ass ways. Maybe it was the difference in our ages, but after years together that shouldn't even matter anymore. I wasn't going to sweat it because whatever happened in this house, stayed in this house. None of this was coming home with me—I'd make sure of that.

Jaylin had gotten up to go into the kitchen to see what Jada was up to. He was watching her cook our food like a hawk, and on a for real tip, I didn't blame him. I laughed when I heard him complaining about how much salt she was shaking into the boiling water. They had started to get into this playful mode with each other and it was kind of interesting. Either he was joking with her or he was attracted to her. I was sure to ask him later.

"Am I doin' this or you?" Jada snapped. "Instead of worryin' yourself about how much salt I'm puttin' into the food, you need to go on back over there and watch the game."

"I'll watch the game, after I get done watching you. Cool out on the fucking salt before that shit kills us."

"Look, fool. As tight as your body is, all you gotta do is add another ten or fifteen more minutes to your workout. A little extra salt ain't gon' kill you."

"You're a bigger idiot than I thought, especially if you believe that adding all that salt to food will not kill you. I'm gon' keep my mouth shut, but when that ass laid up in a casket somewhere, don't be wishing you had listened to me."

Jada sighed and pursed her lips. She shook even more salt into the boiling water. "If I'm gon' be laid up in a casket over salt, you will be, too. You don't have to eat my food, Jaylin, and you're welcome to have an apple, orange or a Little Debbie snack cake for dinner."

Jaylin got up from the stool and went to the fridge to get an apple. He bit into it and then he smacked Jada hard on her ass. She jumped back and playfully poked him with her fork. "Don't play," she said with a grin on her face. "Touch my butt again and I'mma have to cut you."

"Sure," Jaylin said, coming back into the living room and sitting down. "Cut me good, baby, but please cut the salt before you do anything."

Jada threw her hand back at him and continued to work on dinner. The aroma in the kitchen was lit up like an Italian restaurant. She chose to make spaghetti. I was hungry, especially after smoking weed. I had to find something to grub on, and when I got up, I walked by Jaylin.

"Ay," I said, getting his attention. I nodded my head toward Jada. "I think she likes you. My suggestion is to sleep with one eye open."

"Nah, she's down with you. It's in her eyes. Pay attention."

I went into the kitchen and grabbed a bag of Doritos from the pantry. When I closed the door, Jada stood in front of me with a spoonful of sauce in her hand.

"Roc, try this. Let me know if the sauce is too sweet."

"Salty!" Jaylin yelled from afar. "Too damn salty, not sweet."

Jada lifted her middle finger. "Stick it, Jaylin. Far, far up there, okay?"

He laughed.

I tasted the sauce and it was pretty damn good. "It's just right. Can't wait to taste all of it. How much longer before some grub is ready?"

"About ten...fifteen more minutes. I'm glad you liked it."

Something in her eyes said I could have her, and keeping it real, Jada was my kind of woman. So far, I liked her style and she seemed like she could be...fun.

I chilled at the kitchen table eating Doritos. Shortly thereafter, Prince swooped in to holla at me. Sylvia did too, and Chase followed minutes later. Jaylin chilled in the living room.

"Is everybody ready to eat?" Jada said, carrying the pot of cheesy spaghetti to the table. "The cheese garlic bread will be ready in a few minutes, but I'm not puttin' my cookies in the oven until after we eat."

"The spaghetti looks delicious," Sylvia complimented. "Can't wait to taste it." She looked over at Jaylin. "Are you going to join us at the table, Jaylin?"

He lifted the core of the apple he'd finished. "Nah, I'm good. Good luck with that spaghetti. I'm gon' pray that it works out for y'all."

Jada put her hand on her hip and bit down on her lip. She didn't say anything, but Sylvia asked Jaylin to come pray with us. "You don't mind blessing the food with us, do you?"

He got up, and then came over to the table with us. We all stood, but I couldn't remember the last time I said a prayer before eating food. Desa Rae was always getting on me about doing so, but I didn't make it a habit. I went with the flow and held hands with the people next to me, Jada on one side and Prince on the other.

"Close your eyes and bow your heads," Sylvia said. "And Prince, why don't you lead us in prayer."

There was silence and then he spoke up. "Uh, excuse me. But what did you say?"

"I asked that you lead us in prayer."

"Nah, ma, I'm not good with that. Next."

"Roc? How about you?" Sylvia asked.

"I'll pass to Jada."

"Don't be passin' to me. If I say the wrong thing, somebody gon' try to correct me. Besides, I don't like prayin' aloud with other people around. Let Chase say somethin'."

"Okay, y'all." Sylvia sighed from frustration. "Why don't we go around the table and say something that we're thankful for. One at a time and I'll start. Please close your eyes and bow your heads again."

Everybody bowed their heads, but I was peeking and so was Prince.

"Thank you, Lord, for the food we're about to receive," Sylvia said. "Bless Jada for preparing it and please watch over all of us as we take this long journey together for the next three months. Keep us healthy, safe and we pray that we can get along and respect each other. Next."

Chase spoke up. "Thanks for the food and for giving me an opportunity to be in this house with fine men. If you want me with child, now is the time to do it. I thank you in advance. Next."

"Lord, don't let nobody make no babies up in here," Jada said. "But please give me the strength to deal with Jaylin. I pray that I don't have to go upside his head with nothin' made of steel and get arrested. Next."

"I pray the food is good and that Desa Rae will forgive me for bein' in this house with attractive women. Prince."

Jada squeezed my hand and giggled.

"Uh, you died on the cross to save my sins. I sin a lot," Prince said. "Thanks. Next."

"Lord, please bless all the salt that Jada shook over our food," Jaylin said. "Remove it from our bodies, so that we all may live long and healthier lives. Burn the garlic bread in the oven because all of that cheese she used is filled with a bunch of fat and calories. Watch over my children, my Nanny B, my money and keep everything safe while I'm away. Amen."

We all repeated "Amen."

"Now, that wasn't so bad, was it?" Sylvia said as we opened our eyes and sat down at the table. Jaylin returned to his spot on the couch.

"He really works me," Jada griped on her way over to the oven. She opened it, and to her surprise the bread was burned.

"See," Jaylin added with a smile. "When you really need something, all you have to do is pray on it. You need to be banned from the kitchen, woman. Shame on you for serving that shit."

"Oh my God!" Jada shouted. "Really, Jaylin? I can't wait to see what you cook, and just so you know, black folks don't eat cavalier every day like you do."

Chase sucked in a deep breath, then blew it out. "Caviar, sweetie, not cavalier. A cavalier is a vehicle. Besides, I don't know of anyone who wants to eat that every day."

"Correction," Jaylin said. "A cavalier is a horseman, soldier, gentleman or knight. The car is only a representation of the real definition."

"All these damn highly educated people are workin' the shit out of me," Jada said. "Cavalier, caviar, cocacabana…whatever. Jaylin knows what I meant, and, Chase, I'm not your sweetie. Stop sayin' that mess to me, and if you don't appreciate how I pronounce my words, too bad. I don't appreciate that tiny mole on your neck that looks like a booger, but you don't hear me sayin' nothin' about it, do you?"

I felt what Jada was saying, and I was waiting on a motherfucker to correct me on some shit. But while Chase and Jada went back and forth arguing, we grabbed our plates and started to chow down on the food. The spaghetti was dope. I had to give credit where it was due. The woman could cook her ass off. She was proud when we complimented her and boasted about it.

"I can cook that spaghetti with my eyes closed. I can't wait to cook y'all some more stuff, and cookin' is my specialty."

"This is very delicious," Sylvia said as she sucked in a spaghetti noodle. "I like how well you seasoned the meat. The flavors fill the inside of my mouth."

Prince laughed. "Damn, that didn't come out right and my mind shifted in another direction. This is the business, though, Jada. I haven't had a meal like this since my mom cooked it for me. You done scored some points with me."

"Glad y'all like it." Jada blushed and then looked across the room and yelled at Jaylin. "You don't know what you missin'. I know your stomach is mad as hell at you, so why not give it somethin'?"

He ignored Jada, but tightened his fist as New England fumbled the football. Jada picked up her plate from the table and went to go fuck with him. She stood right in front of him, blocking his view from the TV.

"Did you hear what I said?" she asked.

He tried to move her aside, but she didn't budge. He frowned and looked up at her. "Baby, come on now. I'm trying to watch the game."

"I will move out of your way, if you taste my spaghetti. If not, I'm stayin' right here."

Jaylin tried to look around her, but when she moved again, he couldn't see the TV. "Alright. I'm tasting one noodle, that's it."

Jada forked up several noodles and reached out to give the spaghetti to him. He backed away. "Isn't that your fork? I don't know where your mouth has been, and I do not eat after people. If you want me to taste it, get me a clean fork."

Jada shook her head, but went into the kitchen to get a clean fork. When she returned to the living room, she plopped down hard on Jaylin's lap to get his attention.

"Yo ass is heavy," he said, straining and trying to sit up straight. Jada laughed, but didn't move. She used the clean fork to pick up the spaghetti and put it into Jaylin's mouth. He chewed and then swallowed. Afterward, he nodded. "Okay, it's good. Just a tad bit salty, but nonetheless good. Now, get up so I can finish watching the game."

Jada got up, and as any man would do, he checked out her backside. I couldn't tell if he was down with Jada or not, but I was sure of one thing...I could handle her without a doubt.

She proudly walked away from Jaylin, as if he had just given her a blue ribbon for her spaghetti. But she also went off on him, when he asked her to bring him a full plate.

"Nigga, who or what do I look like?" she said. "Your nanny is at home with them kids. I serve no man who don't put money in my pockets, so get up and get your own food."

Jaylin got up, but stopped at the kitchen table. Seriousness washed across his face. "Do not refer to me as a nigga, all right? I have a serious problem with that shit. If you can't control your mouth, don't be mad at me when I start running around here calling you bitches and hoes."

"I know that's right," Chase said, adding her two cents. "It's a respect thing."

Jada put her hand up near Chase's face. "Shut up, tramp. You don't have nothin' to do with this. And Jaylin, you do what you gotta do then. You not my daddy and don't nobody tell me what I can or can't say."

From there, the progress with her, Chase and Jaylin was a wrap. They all went at it, but me, Sylvia and Prince got down on dinner and headed outside to take a swim. Sylvia looked dynamite in her one-piece white swimming suit, and unfortunately for me, my dick had stiffened. I guess the young man in me couldn't control myself. That was a shame, too. I swear I had the best woman that any man could ask for at home waiting for me to return. Desa Rae was all of that and then some. She helped me change my life around and get serious about it. It was because of my relationship with her that I had started to realize life had more to offer than selling drugs on street corners, beefing with niggas and fucking pretty women. We had this Black Love thing going on and switched my thoughts of how spectacular Sylvia looked in her swimming suit, and I thought about how beautiful Desa Rae looked the first time I saw her at a carwash my uncle, Ronnie, owned.

I was working as the manager that day and it was brought to my attention that a woman was in the waiting area, complaining because service was too slow. As I walked up front to find out why the woman was griping, Desa Rae squinted to look at the name on my jumpsuit. Almost immediately, I could tell she liked me, but she was so mad that my good looks were ignored. "Are you the manager?" she asked.

I shrugged because her attitude was kind of annoying. "I'll just say that I'm in charge of things for today. What up?"

She let out a frustrating sigh and kept rolling her eyes without saying anything. If she wasn't willing to talk then I didn't know how to help her. I had plenty of other ways I could help her, and there was something so sexy about how she carried her thickness. Her curves had my palms sweating, and her madness was kind of cute.

"Let me try this again," I said. "How can I help you or do you prefer to stand there with attitude?"

All she did was turn around, sway her hips from side to side, as she made her way to the door. She yanked on it and rushed outside to get into her car. I followed behind her, confused as fuck about why she refused to open her mouth. She had been doing a lot of beefing before I walked up front, now all of a sudden it stopped.

She got into her car and slammed the door. I stood by the driver's side window, scratching my head, but refused to let her go without explaining herself. It looked as if she wasn't going to lower her window, so I knocked on it. She ignored me and put the car in reverse. Unable to go anywhere because a car was in front of her car and behind it, she pounded on the horn. It was apparent that she had some other shit going on in her life. I had never seen anyone so upset over not being able to get their car washed. She took a deep breath and then lowered her window to hear me.

"Are you havin' a postal moment or what? Maybe I should back

away from the car in case I get shot. You too dope to be as angry as you are, and if I've done anything to upset ya, hey, my bad."

She sat silent for a while and tapped her fingers on the steering wheel. It appeared that she was in deep thought, and then she apologized to me for being such a bitch.

"All I want is my car washed. Is that asking too much? I'm on my lunch break, and I have thirty-five minutes left."

I felt kind of bad for her. The fellas had indeed been slacking and it was the third complaint of the day. I pulled on her door handle and offered to personally wash her car for her. She smiled, and then got into my shit about getting inside of her car with my dirty jumpsuit on. I promised not to mess up anything, so she got out of the car and stood in front of me. Her eyes searched me from head to toe and I could tell she was undressing me. I decided to help her out, and instead of keeping the dirty jumpsuit on, I started to remove it.

"You're right about yo car," I said. "I wouldn't want to mess it up."

She stood speechless as I removed the jumpsuit. My zipper had gotten stuck right near my bulge and I asked for her help.

"I'm sure you can handle that," she said. "By the looks of it, I can't."

All I did was laugh, hoping that one day we'd be able to see.

Once I removed the jumpsuit, my biceps full of tattoos worked their magic, and they could be seen by the wife-beater I sported. My jeans hung low on my nicely cut midsection, and Desa Rae looked to be in a trance. She opened her mouth, but not a single word escaped from it. All she did was turn over her keys to me, then she went back inside to wait until I was finished.

I spent the next forty minutes or so cleaning Desa Rae's Lincoln MKS. I could see her watching me through the window. She was biting down on her lip and rubbing her legs. I figured she was thinking about what to do with me or vice versa. Yeah, she looked much older and mature than I was, but so damn what. I'd dated older women before and they were much better than some of the young, airhead chicks I'd hooked up with. She was classy, and there was something about her overall appearance that turned me the fuck on. I couldn't wait to get finished with her car, just so I could ask for her phone number. She would think I was out of my damn mind, and I bet any amount of money, she would say I was too young for her. Too young or not, she wasn't going to leave without me getting those digits. Opportunities like this didn't happen every day, and I saw this as a moment in time that was meant to be.

I was almost finished with Desa Rae's car until my down chick, Vanessa, pulled up in her car and interrupted me. I could see Desa Rae watching us from afar. I tried to pretend as if everything was all good, but I surely didn't want Vanessa hanging around much longer. Money always kept her on the move, so after we talked for a while, I reached into my pocket to hand her some money. Told her to go buy herself something at the mall because I needed to get back to work. She was kind of mad, but just by looking around she could see how busy we really were. I prayed that she wouldn't kiss me, and I was thankful when she got in the car and drove away. After that, I didn't dare look Desa Rae's way again, but a few more minutes later, she came outside and walked up to the car.

"I'm almost done hookin' you up, ma," I said, turning the rag in circles on the windshield. "Feel free to inspect it."

She sashayed around the car, but when she got to the trunk, she stopped and pointed to a little speck on it.

"Looks like you forgot something," she said with a smile on her face.

I rubbed the tiny spot with a towel. "There. Is that better? And if you look hard enough, there is a chance that you may see many more of those specks."

"I hope not, especially since I need to know how much this is going to cost me. If you know you didn't do a good job, maybe you should offer me a discount or something."

I wanted to offer her more than a discount, but I would save my offer for another time. I tucked the rag into my back pocket and sat my backside against the trunk.

"If I put in work like that, I usually don't offer discounts. But I do have another idea in mind. Do you care to know what it is?"

"Idea? What kind of idea?"

I told her it was simple and that all I wanted to know was her name. That was when she told me it was Desa Rae. Keeping the conversation going, I wasted no time asking for her digits. All she did was laugh and then she inquired about my age.

"I'm twenty-four."

"What?" she shouted. "Oh, no. Boy, let me stop playing with you and get out of here. I really need to get going."

She looked into her purse for money, but when she reached out to hand it to me, I wouldn't take it. I teased her about not telling me how old she was and about her trying to jet after I told her my age.

"I know what it is," I said. "You're afraid because you know you can't handle me. That's a shame too, because I know damn well that I can handle you."

"Just so you know, I am forty years old. There is no way I would ever hook up with a man your age. It was nice meeting you, though, and if you don't take this money, I'm going to assume that you washed my car for free."

"I prefer your number."

"And I prefer not to give it to you. So goodbye, handsome. Maybe in another lifetime, but surely not this one."

Desa Rae drove off, but I could see her eyeing me in the rearview mirror. I didn't know why I let her get away so easily, but there was something inside of me that knew I'd see her again.

A week later, I saw Desa Rae at a nightclub. That was when she allowed me to drive her home, and after convincing her for several weeks that age was just a number, we hooked up and the two of us have been on a roll ever since. But now, what I had built with the woman I loved was being challenged more than it had ever been before. After all we'd been through, I thought I was ready to be married, but I couldn't figure out why I was considering making moves with the chicks in this house, especially Chase. There was a little something about her that intrigued the shit out of me.

Chase

I had a confession to make. I wanted a piece of him—Jaylin. Behind all that arrogance and hardness was a gentle man who knew how to care for and take care of a woman. I could see it between his thighs—I mean eyes. All he needed was for the wall he had put up to be broken down. There was a side to him that was funny, sexy and very playful. He didn't want anyone to notice it, but I did. The way his lips moved when he talked made me want to suck them into mine. He walked with so much confidence; I liked that about him. As he sat back on the couch and watched television, I liked the way he moved his shirt aside and rubbed his chest. Loved the way he looked down at his manhood and adjusted himself. His bulge didn't seem like it would be easy to tackle, but I was ready to play. I had to change the way I'd been doing things and get on the right track. That started here and right now. I still wanted a piece of the Roc, too, but he came easy. Too easy. There would be no challenge in getting what I wanted from him and his eyes said that I could have him whenever I wanted to. That would be soon.

Now that Jada and Jaylin were at it again, I decided to make my move. For a minute there, I thought he actually liked her, but then again, I should've known better. A man of his stature would never stoop low and pursue a ghetto, out-of-shape slut like Jada.

She couldn't even get out one sentence that made sense. Surely it was driving him nuts, as it was me. When she sat her big ass on top of Jaylin, I thought she would break him. He should've pushed her hood-living self on the floor and called it a day. The only thing she had me beat on was cooking. I couldn't cook worth nothing, but when the time came for me to do it, I had to make sure it was right. The body that Jaylin had required healthy foods to go into it. I knew he would appreciate my efforts and consideration for serving him foods that weren't dripping with grease and filled with sugar.

Jada and Sylvia were outside near the swimming pool, but the men were in the game room. I was in the bathroom putting on a two-piece metallic gold bikini. It barely covered my butt and my meaty breasts peeked outside of my top. I brushed my hair into a sleek ponytail and then slid into my flip-flops so I could show Jaylin, as well as Roc, what I was working with. Prince was an attractive young man as well, but he was too young. He had to be in his early twenties, maybe even younger than that. I didn't get down like that, but I was sure to watch my belongings, just in case he tried to steal something from me.

Walking as if I were a runway model, I strutted outside to see what was up. A song by Drake was blasting through the loud speakers and I was surprised to see Sylvia chatting it up with Roc. He looked fabulous with his shirt off. Talk about a man having it all together—he surely did. I didn't see Jaylin or Prince, until I walked further onto the patio and saw that they were still in the game room. Jada sat on one of the lounge chairs reading a book. Hopefully, it would help to enhance her vocabulary.

As I sauntered over to the table where Roc and Sylvia sat, I could see the lust in Roc's eyes. His white swimming trunks against all that black looked dynamite on him. Sylvia had a look of jealousy in her eyes, but if she was going to compete with me, she should've jazzed up her plain one-piece swimming suit before coming out here. I mean, she was decent, but I didn't see her as a threat at all. I sat right next to Roc, who I still considered my baby's daddy.

"Look at those arms," I said, squeezing his biceps. Solid as a rock—he was definitely representing. "What does it take to have arms like that?"

"A lot of workin' out," he said. "But you should already know that. Your body ain't short stoppin'."

No, it wasn't. I was glad he noticed. Sylvia looked uneasy. She pulled her braids over to one shoulder and rubbed her hair. "I'm going to go get me something to drink," she said. "Would either of you like for me to bring you something?"

"I'll get up in a minute to see what's up," Roc said to her.

"If you see any wine coolers in there, please bring me one," I said.

She walked away, and I noticed Roc checking her out. I placed my finger on his cheek, turning his face toward me. "So," I said. "What's the play? Tell me some things about yourself, Roc. Are you a single man?"

He licked his lips and rubbed the flowing waves on his head. "I'm down with somebody, but she be funny actin' sometimes. What about you? Or does any of that really matter, especially since we're here and they're wherever?"

I shrugged my shoulders. "I'm single and loving it. I just didn't want to cause any setbacks in your relationship, that's all."

"No worries. Nobody can setback my relationship, but me. Now riddle me this. You sayin' all of this because you want to hook up, right?"

"If that's how you want to put it, yes, hooking up sounds

appropriate. So whenever you're done getting a feel for Sylvia, and I'm sure she'll disappoint you, I'll be in the pool. I'm hot right now and need to cool off."

Saying nothing else, I walked away and jumped into the bubbling swimming pool with plenty of underwater lighting. The whole area was cozy and I couldn't wait for Roc to join me. Jaylin seemed occupied, and now he was in the weight room with Prince. Looked like they were showing each other a few techniques, and I could see them laughing. Jada had finally put her book down and she was sitting at the edge of the pool with her feet in the water. She had on a one-piece swimming suit with a pair of shorts covering her bottom half. Poor thing. I guess her weight didn't matter, since she was also snacking on those chocolate chip cookies she'd baked earlier.

Sylvia returned to the table, but after a short while I saw her go back inside. That was when Roc jumped his sexy self into the water and swam over to me. It was a wet and wonderful sight.

"Why you out here floatin'? You should be swimmin'," he said.

"I was waiting on you. I didn't want to go into the deep water, unless you were with me."

Roc turned his back and gestured for me to get on it. I straddled my legs around him and pressed my breasts against his back so he could feel them. He was so strong. The way his body felt made my pussy dance. I hoped he couldn't feel it doing the pop, as he swam around the water with me on his back. I laughed a little, joked a lot, and when he lifted me in the air, I screamed.

"Roc, please don't drop me," I begged. "This water is too deep and I can't swim!"

"Yes, you can," he said. "You just playin' with me and lyin' to me, too."

He tossed me several inches away from him, but made sure that

I didn't go far underneath the water. I threw my arms around his neck, and, this time, I straddled the front of him. I could feel his hardness pressing into the right place. And after not having sex for almost two months, I was so ready to let him dip into it. I wasn't the type of woman who had to wait to do these things and one-night stands were what I lived by. It was rare that I would ever get attached to a man, and the ones that I wanted, I had no problem going after. I wanted Roc and I wanted Jaylin. He and Prince had finally come out of the workout area and were now chilling back in the lounge chairs drinking. I didn't know what the two of them possibly had in common; they were like night and day. But I saw Jaylin peeping Roc and me a few times. This was my chance to show him that I wasn't only interested in him, even though I was sure he was confident I was.

I gazed into Roc's eyes as he held me and nodded my head toward the stone-layered waterfalls. "Would you like to go behind there?" I said.

"What's shakin' behind there?"

"My ass, if you want it to be. But why don't you follow me and find out?"

I broke away from Roc and swam behind the waterfall where there was a cozy and secluded area with dimmed lighting. I wished something more romantic was playing in the background, but the lyrics by Kanye West had to do.

Roc swam in behind me. I wasted no time going up to him and pressing my body against his. I rested my arms on his shoulders and looked into his serious eyes that showed interest, but a little hesitation.

"This is so much better, isn't it?" I said, referring to our private surroundings.

"Yeah, it's cool."

In an effort to break the disconnect, I leaned in to kiss him, but he resisted and backed his head up.

"Check this," he said. "I'm not sure if I'm really down with what you bringin' or not. I'm here to have some fun, no doubt, but I didn't expect to be movin' in this direction with nobody so soon."

"I get that, Roc, really I do, but I'm letting you know now that I'm not going to let up on you. I'm not asking you for a commitment or anything like that. All I'm interested in is, quite frankly, sex. Sex that I know you wouldn't mind having with me, so take a day or two to think about it. Whenever you're ready, we can meet right back here."

There was no doubt in my mind that Roc was in love with someone. But I was in need of him. He had a choice to make, and I helped him to quickly make up his mind when I lowered my hand inside of his swim trunks. I circled my hand around his shaft and felt it swell to its full potential.

"Wow," I said as my eyes grew bigger. "That's pretty big."

His eyelids lowered, and I could tell he was appreciating my touch. "Yeah, it is. And, I, uh, I...I wish you wouldn't do that."

"But I want to," I said, whispering in his ear. "I want to feel all of this inside of me. I'm so wet right now, Roc. Don't you want to feel me, too?"

I was working the tip of his thick head over, leaving him near speechless. He swallowed hard, then closed his eyes. I felt his body get tense, but that was when his eyes shot open and he put pressure on my hand. "Let it go," he said in a hurry. "Chill out."

I slowly released it, watching as Roc sighed from relief. "I'm out," he said to me and then swam away. For whatever reason, he stopped and turned toward me. "Meet me in the game room in about fifteen minutes. I don't want us to start nothin' we can't finish."

That left a wide smile on my face. I waited for a few minutes before I left from behind the waterfall to join the others. Trying to pass by the time, I kicked up a conversation with Jada who couldn't even hold one with me. We were very much on different levels, especially since all she talked about was her numerous marriages and her lousy-ass girlfriends. I was glad to get away from her, and fifteen minutes later, I excused myself from our conversation and went into the game room with Roc who was already inside shooting pool. He was bending over the pool table, getting ready to take a shot.

"Do you play?" he asked. "If so, go get a stick."

I sauntered up to him and reached my hand out to touch his stick. "Got it. Now, what do you want me to do with it? I'm ready to play whenever you are."

Roc smiled, but removed my hand from exploring his growing muscle. "Ma, you got that mutha clownin', but the stick I was referrin' to was the stick over there."

Roc pointed to the row of pool sticks against the wall.

"Oh," I said in a teasing manner. "Those sticks. I thought you meant something else, but I guess I can figure out something else to do with the sticks on the wall."

I walked away to remove one of the pool sticks from the wall. I watched as Roc took his shot and then he motioned his hand for me to proceed. When I did, you'd better believe that I stepped my sexiness up a notch. The metallic bikini was already working wonders for me, but I bent over right in front of Roc to take my shot. Before I did, I turned my head to the side, just to be sure that his eyes were on me. They were focused in like a laser, and the turning of my head didn't even break his trance. I couldn't help but to make my ass jiggle and my moves made him laugh.

"You know you wrong for fuckin' with me like that, but it's all good. Don't be mad at me when you mess around and hurt yourself."

"You can be sure that I'm looking forward to it. How many times do I have to say it before you start to believe me?"

I took the shot and purposely missed so Roc could come over to offer his assistance. I suspected that he would, and it didn't take long for him to come up to the table and show me the ropes.

"Hold the stick like this." He pulled the stick back and forth, gliding it on the table to take a shot. He did, and to no surprise, the ball went into the hole.

"Thanks for showing me, but I never thought that I was holding sticks incorrectly. I guess we learn something new every day, huh?"

Roc knew exactly what "sticks" I was referring to. "You may very well know how to work with some sticks in particular, just not that stick you have in your hand."

I winked at him, and yet again, I purposely missed the next shot. "Damn-it," I said. "If you don't mind, I think you may have to come closer to help me with this stick. It's not cooperating."

Roc was no fool. The look on his face implied that he knew what I was up to, yet he had no problem falling in line with my games. He stood behind me, moving my arms and hands in the correct position to hold the stick. There was too much breathing room between us, so I backed my ass up to touch him. He, however, moved back and stood with his arms folded across his chest.

"Why are you jumping back like I'm contagious or something?" I asked. "I promise I won't bite, unless you allow me to. And even then, I'll be gentle."

Roc rubbed his chin, studying me. "Ay, riddle me this, ma. Are you always this aggressive with men or is it just somethin' about me that got you fired up like this?"

I had to laugh. "Fired up? That would be a mild way of putting it, but to answer your questions, no, I'm not always this aggressive, and it takes a certain kind of man to move me. I mean, have you looked in the mirror lately? You can't stand there displaying all those muscles with those white trunks on and expect not to get a reaction from me. I'm only reacting to how I feel in the presence of a very handsome man. Anything wrong with that?"

"Not at all. Now, turn back around and let me react to you takin' your next shot. I'll let you know if I approve or not."

I faced the pool table and bent far over. With my legs slightly spread, I took the shot. This time my ball went in.

I remained in position, and turned my head to look at Roc. "Yay to me for getting the ball in. What you got to say about that?"

Roc stepped forward, this time leaving no space between us. I could feel his hard dick against my ass, and there was no secret that I was more than ready to fuck him. He had the nerve to tease me by grinding just enough to make me feel more of him. That was when I stood up straight and placed the stick on the pool table. Roc's arm eased around my waist and he rubbed my stomach to put me at ease. The only reason I had tensed up was because I was surprised by his actions.

"Turn around," he said to me.

I faced him, and he lifted me on the pool table. As I sat near the edge with my legs opened, he moved in between them.

"A chick who got my dick this hard must straight up be about somethin'. But let me put my cards on the table right now. I don't want there to be no misunderstandings between us. I'm engaged to a very beautiful woman who don't need no more headaches from me. There is no question that if I weren't engaged, I would lay you back on this table and get down to some for real business. But—"

I placed my finger on Roc's lips to silence him. "There is no need for you to say another word. Let's not get too serious about this, and you know what, Roc? If sex between us happens, then it just happens. Whatever is meant to be will be, and the fact that you are engaged will not change my thoughts of wanting to hook up with you."

Not saying another word, I leaned in for a kiss and Roc reciprocated. Our hands started to move into action, and the first place I touched was his ass. I squeezed it and then pushed it in, so he could be closer to my heat. His dick poked at my goods, and all either of us had to do was slide the crotch of my bikini bottoms aside to expose my pussy. Roc massaged my thighs, and as we broke away from our juicy kiss, I sat back on my elbows. His eyes did a quick scan down my near flawless body, and all he could do was shake his head.

"Yo sexy ass gon' get me in trouble," he confessed. "Big trouble, so I'mma need to stay far, far away from you. So, do me a favor and don't take it personal, all right?"

I didn't know if I should take him serious or not. But since we were in such a playful mood, I pouted. "I won't take it personal, but my feelings will be a tiny bit bruised. You don't want to hurt my feelings, do you?"

"Never." Roc bent over and placed a soft, delicate kiss on my flat stomach. He licked his tongue down to my navel and inched down even further. He stopped right above the edge of my bikini line. "Let's go back into the swimmin' pool area. It's gettin' too damn heated in here, and I don't know if I'll be able to restrain myself much longer."

Seeing that Roc was trying his best to fight this, I removed myself from the table and headed to the door with him by my side. There was too much chemistry between us, and even though sex didn't occur with us tonight, I was sure that it was bound to happen soon.

I misjudged Prince. I should've known better because I always came down hard on people who judged me. The brotha had been misguided, no doubt, but he had a good head on his shoulders. At twenty-three-years old, he was a businessman, trying to make things happen. Trying to pull himself out of the ghetto, and I admired that about him. I could tell there was hustling going on and that he had difficult struggles along the way. We all had them, however, in this world, only the strong survived.

After we got finished testing out the workout equipment, we sat on the patio and had a few drinks. I had Remy and Prince had Patron. After a while, he said he wasn't feeling well, so he turned in for the night. I overheard Sylvia and Jada talking about a book Jada was reading, and I saw Roc and Chase having a good time in the game room. It looked as if things got a li'l heated, and I was surprised to see him come out of the game room so soon.

"Can't believe everybody still up," he said, taking a seat next to me and putting his hands behind his head. "It's almost one o'clock in the mornin', ain't it?"

"Almost. Prince the only one who shut it down because he had a headache."

"A headache from smokin' all that weed. That nigga ain't 'sleep. He probably in there goin' through people's shit."

I wasn't worried because I brought a tiny safe that I kept my valuables and money in. Nobody knew where I placed it and it was in a very good hiding place.

"He was high as a kite," I said. "But you ain't trying to talk about the next man, are you?"

"My high flew out the window, as soon as Chase started sweatin' me and makin' moves. I gotta get my head on straight before I fuck up."

"Chase has been making moves all day. I'm surprised you weren't ready. She seems like the kind of woman who has no problem going after what she wants."

"I'm feelin' that too," Roc said, stroking his chin as he kept his eyes locked on Chase from a distance. Her ass was so nice and round that it swallowed her bikini bottoms. Pussy looked pretty fat too, and if a man didn't know any better, he'd be fucked up.

"Good night, boys," she said, walking by us. "Don't stay up too late, and, Jaylin, I'm loving those red swimming trunks. What a good look on you?"

Neither one of us responded. Roc rubbed his hands together, looking as if something heavy was on his mind. "I'm getting ready to go harass Jada and see what Sylvia is up to," I said. "Don't let Chase get into your head, man, and if you got straight love at home, don't fuck it up. It ain't always worth it. I'm speaking from experience."

Roc pounded my fist and headed inside. I then got up to go holler at the ladies. They were now playing cards.

"Get up," I said to Jada.

She cocked her head back. "What? Why do I need to get up?"

"Because you're sitting on something."

She got up to look, and I rushed to sit in her seat. Before she started bitching, I pulled her back and sat her on my lap. She resisted a little, but she smirked and got comfortable.

"Why you take my seat?" she asked.

"Because I know you're losing this game and I came to help you beat Sylvia."

"Well, you're too late," Sylvia said. "I'm only twenty points away from winning this game and Jada is in the negative."

"Just deal the cards," I said to Sylvia. "Let us see what cards we get before you go calling yourself a winner."

Sylvia dealt the cards. Jada and I looked through her hand and it wasn't about nothing. She had two spades. That was it.

"I quit." Jada pouted. "You win, but there is always tomorrow. Right now, I'm goin' to bed." She slightly turned to face me. "Jaylin, you gon' come tuck me in?"

"Only if you promise not to call me a nigga again and you make me a healthy meal that I can eat."

Jada put her hand on her hip. "I can't promise you all that, and as much as you complained about my spaghetti, you ate the shit out of it. So stop playin' and come tuck me in."

"I will, once I get done talking to Sylvia. Don't wait up for me, though."

I winked at Jada as she playfully rolled her eyes and went into the house.

"What is it with you and Jada?" Sylvia questioned. "Are the two of you liking each other?"

"She's not my type, but she's sweet. She wanna be hard, but I bet she wouldn't hurt a fly."

Sylvia laughed. "I would have to disagree with you on that. Jada looks as if she don't play, so you'd better watch yourself messing with her."

"Maybe so."

There was silence for a while, and then I suggested going for a swim.

"I would love to, Jaylin, but I can't swim. Never learned how to and all I ever do is just get my feet wet."

"Well, sit on the steps in the water and get wet. You can watch me swim. Maybe by then you'll figure out where you know me from."

Sylvia stood and removed the sheer wrap from around her waist. She walked in front of me and my evaluation process clicked in. Sexy—check. Nails done—check. Hair intact—check. Great personality—check. Nice ass—check. Pretty titties—check. The only thing that I didn't like was a huge birthmark on her thigh. She couldn't do anything about that, so I didn't hold it against her. She held the rail and stepped into the water. When she sat back on the steps, the water came up to her waist. She watched as I jumped in and went under to knock off the chill I thought I'd get from entering the water. It was warm, though, and felt very relaxing.

I wiped the water from my face and then went for a quick swim, stroking my way up and down the pool. Sylvia started kicking her feet in the water and that was when I swam up to her. I sat in between her legs and she started to massage my back and shoulders. Her deep massage was working wonders.

"Now, that shit feels good. What you got on your hands?"

"Water," she said, laughing. "But you are real, real tense."

I cocked my neck from side to side and then rolled it in circles. "So, have you had enough time to think about where you know me from?" I said.

"Been thinking about it all day. Just can't figure it out, but I do know for a fact that there was no intimacy between us."

"Are you positive about that?"

"One hundred and twenty percent positive."

"What makes you so sure?"

"Because I would remember if a man like you were ever inside of me."

I removed her hand from my shoulder and turned around. "What do you mean by a man like me?"

"I mean a man as sexy, handsome and well-endowed down below as you are. As bright as you seem to be and I'm impressed. Don't think for one minute that I'm not paying attention."

"And you should be. For the record, I am too."

I held myself up, while looking down at Sylvia underneath me. She rested on her elbows and her legs were wide open as I was in between them. The direction of my eyes dropped to her lips, but before I could inch forward, she lifted her head and pecked my lips. "Jaylin, I'm here to deal with my pain. I've made some mistakes with a relationship that I'm not happy about. Just felt as if I needed to tell you that."

"That makes two of us, so what's your purpose for telling me that?"

"I'm not interested in having a relationship with anybody right now. I'm not capable of giving you what you may need, no matter what that may be."

"I'm not interested in a relationship either, but you are most certainly capable of giving me what I need. You're giving it to me right now."

Sylvia held my head steady, as our tongues lightly danced in each other's mouths. Her kiss was sweet, gentle and was what I needed right now. I squeezed her hips and eased my hand between her legs to touch her goodies. I could feel her soft hairs; she didn't have much. But when I attempted to slip my finger inside of her, she tightened her legs.

"Not right here, Jaylin," she whispered.

"Then where?"

"I...I don't know. Someplace where there are no cameras."

It must have clicked for us at the same time—the bathroom. We hurried out of the swimming pool and rushed to the bathroom. I had Sylvia hemmed up against the closed door, while I grinded hard against her.

"I can feel it, Jaylin," she confirmed, barely able to take a breath as we smacked lips. "Your dick is so big. I can't wait to ride it, taste it, umm," she moaned.

I lowered the top of her swimming suit and went to work on her sweet, chocolate breasts. As I massaged and sucked them, I also worked her tiny nipples with the curled tip of my tongue. Sylvia squirmed against the door. She was on the tips of her toes, trying hard to control her trembles.

"It's tingling." She referred to her pussy. "Make it stop, Jaylin, please make it stop."

"I don't want it to stop, baby, I want it to come. You gon' come all over me, right?"

"I'd rather show you than tell you."

My dick was so hard that I yanked my trunks off, lowering them to the floor. Sylvia gripped my ass and dug her nails deep into my butt. Then, her hands ran through my wet hair like she needed this more than me. A change, that is. Something new. Something that had no emotional attachments. Something that wouldn't hurt me like I was hurt when I found out my ex-wife, Nokea, had been having sex with another man. And even though we weren't married anymore, I could have killed her that day. To hell with my thoughts of marrying her again. Never would I do that shit again because she had lied to me for many months. It was over and I was not a forgiving man. I was free to be who I wanted to be. Free to fuck anybody I wanted to and free of the love that I tried to convince myself, over and over again, that I didn't want anymore.

Sylvia knocked me out of my thoughts when she pushed me

backward. I staggered, but watched as she stepped out of the rest of her swimming suit. She backed up to me, ass first, and positioned my dick right between her legs. I could feel her heat, even before I entered.

"You're going to love this," she said, bending over in front of me. I moved her long braids aside and began to rub her smooth back. My dick was in position to aim then shoot, but as soon as I separated her round ass cheeks, Sylvia caught me off guard.

"Oh. My. God," she cried out and rose up a bit. "I...I remember where I know you from."

I pulled her back toward me. "Fuck! Tell me later. I'm not interested in knowing that right now."

She jumped away from me as if I were contagious. "Jonathan Taylor," she said, snapping her finger. "You know him, don't you?"

It took a few seconds, but hell, yes, I knew John-John. He was a close lawyer friend of mine. "Yes, I know him. He was married to Dana for years and—"

I turned around and let out a deep sigh. My dick deflated when I remembered Sylvia was his secretary, whom he had fallen in love with. "Damn," I said, turning to face her. "I remember now. I came to the office to see him a few times and you were there."

She smiled, but looked embarrassed. "Yep, that would've been me. I remember you too. My coworkers and I couldn't stop talking about you that day."

"Well, that's too bad," I said with another sigh.

I was damn sure disappointed that we had to pack it up, but I couldn't even see myself getting down with a woman who had truly meant something to one of my partners. I swiped my trunks from the floor and handed Sylvia her swimming suit. She sighed too.

"I am so mad right now," she said. "A little embarrassed too, and I hope you don't think—"

"Doesn't matter what I'm thinking right now, but you'd better hurry up and get out of this bathroom before I say to hell with Jonathan. Besides, I need a cold shower right now. I doubt that you want to be in here with me."

Sylvia covered herself with one of the towels and then put her swimming suit back on. She kissed my cheek, before leaving the bathroom and closing the door behind her. Yeah, I was pissed, but hopefully the cold shower would do me some good. I put it on full blast and then stepped inside to wash myself. I lathered my entire body and closed my eyes in thought. As I had done many times before, I visualized that motherfucker touching Nokea's body. I could see him sucking her breasts and going in and out of her pussy as if it belonged to him. I wanted details; details that she wouldn't give me. Details that she said were none of my business anymore. I was left to assume a lot. Was he capable of making her come, and what did she say to him in the moment? I was sick to my fucking stomach about the whole thing, but she didn't care. All she did was throw up in my face all the shit I had done to her. Rightfully so, I guessed, but we both knew that taking care of our children was the priority. Nothing else mattered anymore, and if we were to ever have a future together again, it would be far into the future because there was no getting over the lies anytime soon.

My dick was still hard, so I reached down to touch it. Thought about what had happened between Sylvia and me and what a big mistake that would've been. I really didn't have a choice but to use my hand, but as I started to work myself, the bathroom door flew open. Jada stood in the doorway, but she let out a loud gasp and grabbed her chest. I rushed out of the shower and quickly tied a white towel around my waist.

"Damn, baby, are you alright?" I asked as I made my way up to her. She held onto the doorknob and eased to the ground. Her body was shaking like she was in a convulsion-like state, and she kept choking and gagging at the same time. I assumed she was having a heart attack, so I lay her back on the floor so I could perform CPR and give her mouth-to-mouth resuscitation. With all the noise, everyone rushed out of the bedroom to see what was going on.

"Oh, my," Sylvia said, rushing over to us. "Is she going to be okay?"

"All that salt," Prince joked, but I didn't see anything funny.

But as I was about to pump Jada's chest, her eyes popped open and she grabbed my arms. "Please, please tell me, Jaylin. Is it really that humongous? Did I really see what I think I saw with my own eyes? Are you seriously packin' like that? Really?"

I was so mad that I pushed her away from me and stood up. Some people laughed, as I walked to the bedroom and slammed the door behind me. I went into the closet and pressed my hands against the wall. I couldn't help it that thoughts of Nokea had rushed across my mind when I was in the bathroom getting ready to have sex with Sylvia. If I couldn't be with the one I loved, in a way that I wanted to be with her, then I would never show love for anyone else. I told Nokea the same thing that day, but she wasn't trying to hear it.

Nokea and I had been getting along well, especially considering that our marriage had fallen apart. I had given her the space she'd asked for, and I refused to force her to do anything she wasn't comfortable with doing. She was still trying to heal from my adulterous ways that wound up costing us big time. I understood her need to back away, and as long as we remained great parents to our children, I was good. We continued to live separately and it appeared not to be a problem for either of us. I had gotten accustomed to Nokea not being in the same house as me, but I'd be lying if I said I didn't miss rolling over in the morning and seeing her beautiful face. But I'd made my bed and was willing to lay in it. That was what I told myself, until I drove to Nokea's place that day with Nanny B and the kids. I was supposed to drop the kids off and take Nanny B to the doctor for a checkup. But when I arrived at Nokea's condo, something didn't seem right. It took her about five minutes to open the door, and when she did, the look in her eyes said it all. She was nervous about something, and her slouchy clothes and disheveled hair implied that she was in the midst of getting her fuck on. The kids rushed inside to hug her, but with her eyes still locked on me, she asked why we were so early.

"Does it matter?" I asked, then stepped inside. My eyes roamed the dining room and the living room as well. Nanny B came inside too, but she remained by the door with me.

"It doesn't matter," Nokea said. "But you're two hours early. Had I known you were coming this soon, I would have made other arrangements."

I wasn't so sure what kind of other arrangements Nokea was talking about until I saw a tall, brown-skinned brotha with dreads come from the kitchen with no shoes on. My face fell flat, and my gaze was without a blink. Nokea and I had been getting our fuck on every now and then, and I was shocked that she had started seeing someone else. She told me that her schedule was too busy for her to be dating, and that if she did start seeing someone, she would let me know. Obviously, that wasn't the case, and she could tell by the look in my eyes that I wasn't too pleased about the brotha being there. Like always, Nokea turned to Nanny B for assistance. "Would you mind taking the kids outside on the playground for a while?"

Nanny B side-eyed the brotha on the couch who hadn't said one word, and then she told the kids to come with her. After they left, I walked by Nokea and went into the living room to introduce myself. I extended my hand to the brotha and he stood up. No smile was on his face, but a *smirk was definitely there. It was apparent that he knew who I was.*

"And you are?" I asked while shaking his hand.

Nokea rushed to speak before he did. "Jaylin, this is Tyrese. He's one of the distributors for my new clothing line."

"Nice to meet you, Jaylin. I've heard a lot about you."

"Too bad I can't say the same."

I let go of his hand, walked away and started to stroke my goatee. My insides were boiling. I tried to show Nokea that I was a changed man and could handle her dating other people, especially since I'd been dipping into some other things from time to time. Nothing serious because I knew only one woman had my heart.

Nokea cleared her throat and asked Tyrese if he was getting ready to leave.

"Yes, sweetheart, but I can't find my keys. Have you seen them?"

"They're on the dining room table, next to the wineglasses," I said.

He thanked me and then walked over to the table to get his keys. Nokea followed and I turned away because if she kissed him upon departure, I would have to break her fucking neck. And then the whole sweetheart bullshit had me on edge. I was pissed off, and it looked like some kind of celebration had taken place this morning or last night. I suspected last night; when I went into her room, several burned candles were on the nightstand with wineglasses. Her silk black panties were on the floor, and when I went into the bathroom, there were two condoms in the trashcan. The shower didn't look wet, but a hint of sex was fumigating the room. I heard the front door close, and minutes later, Nokea appeared in the doorway. She could barely look at me, as I sat calmly on the bed with her panties in my hand.

"Tell me why you never mentioned to me that you were seeing someone else, and how long has this been going on?" I asked.

Nokea didn't know how to read me, so she stayed by the doorway, in case I broke out in one of my rages.

"I didn't tell you because I didn't want to hurt your feelings. I knew how difficult it would be for you to accept me dating someone else, but now that you know, I've been seeing him for about four or five months."

I sucked my teeth, while at the same time my flesh was crawling. Goose bumps appeared on my arms and the lump in my throat could not be swallowed. The thoughts of another man making love to her were eating me alive. I didn't know how I would be able to deal with this shit going forward. Now, I couldn't even look at her, and I preferred to keep my eyes fixated on the floor.

"Has he ever been around our kids?" I asked. I hoped to hell that he hadn't because that was the one thing I would never tolerate.

"No. Never. That's why I'm a little disappointed that you brought them over this early. Had I known, I would have made Tyrese leave sooner. I'm not ready to introduce him to our children just yet because it's not that serious."

"But it's serious enough for you to give your pussy to him, huh? If you wanted sex, why didn't you call me?"

This time, I lifted my head to look at her and awaited an answer.

"Because I'm attracted to Tyrese, and I wanted to have sex with him. I told you before, Jaylin, that I wasn't going to put my life on hold for you. You agreed that I shouldn't, but I get a feeling that you don't approve of this."

God knows I was trying to remain calm about this and not upset her. I also knew what I'd said, but that was before I saw this shit with my own eyes.

I laid Nokea's panties on the bed and walked up to her. I lifted her chin because she had looked down. Our gaze into each other's eyes was intense, but I had to be truthful with her about what I was feeling.

"I don't approve of this shit, and I will never approve of it, especially when you entice motherfuckers in the panties I bought you, when you wine and dine them with champagne bought with my money, when you *fuck them in the same bed you fuck me in, and when you allow them to taste your pussy that I tasted less than two weeks ago. So, hell no, I don't approve, and I advise you to rethink this shit. If not, I see much hell lurking in your future, and I'm just being honest."*

I walked off, but Nokea reached for my arm to halt my steps.

"When does it stop, Jaylin? Why won't you be happy for me like you said you would be? We tried…for years we tried and it didn't work out like we had planned for it to. We owe ourselves—"

I shook my head from side to side and reached out to squeeze her face in my hands. I may have held it tighter than I was supposed to, but that was because I couldn't control my anger as much as I had hoped to.

"No. We tried and we are going to keep on trying. You can't fuck the love we have for each other away by being with another man. You've been there and done that before. So have I, with other women, and the one thing nobody will ever do is strip you from me. They are welcomed to anything else, but not you. You can call me selfish, controlling or whatever you want to, but your relationship with Tyrese ends today. I'm giving you one week to give that motherfucker his walking papers, and I expect a phone call from you, telling me that it's over. One week, Nokea, that's it."

Taking a deep breath to calm myself, I pecked her lips. That pained me to do, especially since I had an idea as to where her lips had been. I silently counted to ten and did as I had learned to do in these situations—walk away.

"You're not going to have it your way, Jaylin. Not this time. I won't allow it."

I didn't even bother to turn around, but I meant what I'd said. "We'll have to see about that, baby. And don't you ever forget what I'm made of."

When the next week rolled around, Nokea showed me what she was made of. She ignored every last one of my calls, and when she did eventually speak to me, she made it clear that Tyrese was there to stay. Almost six months later, he was still in the picture. I had somehow learned to cope. I had also came face-to-face with the true meaning of "don't dish it out if you can't take it." But when all was said and done, I was confident that Nokea and I would grow old together. A year later, Tyrese was history, but the rejection that I'd felt from Nokea's lengthy relationship with him left me bitter.

So what, I faked a heart attack. But after seeing Jaylin's hands holding that *thing*, I knew he was capable of breaking a bitch down with that mutha hanging between his legs. He was mad at me, but ask me if I cared. Eventually, he'd get over it, just as I had done with the numerous arguments we'd had.

Honestly, I had gotten to like his silly self. I was the only person in this house capable of killing him with kindness. Behind all that hardness was a man who liked to have fun. I saw it from the moment I laid eyes on him, and, at first, I wasn't interested in screwing him or anything like that. The crush I had was on Roc, but I wanted to see how this thing with him and Chase was going to play out. Now, I wasn't so sure if I cared about that. Jaylin's dick looked delicious, and I'd be a fool not to at least try to get a piece of it.

Then again—all BS aside—I wasn't no dick-hungry chick. I talked a lot of bull, but if or when it ever came down to the real deal, I wasn't sure if I would put up a thing. For now, the most important thing to me was winning this challenge. I was a fighter and I always played to win. It would be tough getting rid of the men in this house, but the women were easy. All they had their minds wrapped around was dick, and when Sylvia came into the bedroom last night, I was so sure she had given Jaylin a piece of it. That was why he was in the shower; he was washing the sex smell off of him. That nasty heifer, Sylvia, came straight to bed without washing her ass. That was trifling.

I tossed and turned all night and was unable to go back to sleep. It was after three in the morning and there I was up, staring at the ceiling in my cotton, Tweety Bird pajamas. Roc was next to me knocked the hell out and Chase was in the bed beside him with her short negligee on, trying to get noticed. That sucker was cut right below her coochie, and she had the nerve to have on a thong. Prince's ghetto self was over there snoring loudly, but I didn't hear a peep out of Jaylin. Sylvia was in the bed next to him, and I'm sure she was happy about that.

I punched my pillow a few times, trying to make it more comfortable. Cleared the mucus from my throat and then coughed.

"Why don't you take yo ass to sleep?" Jaylin said from across the room. "Why you moving around so much?"

I sat up and put the pillow on my lap. "Because this room is too dark, and I think I see dead people. Can I come lay in the bed with you?"

"Hell fucking naw. This bed ain't big enough for the two of us."

"Yes, it is," I said, stomping out of my bed and walking over to his. "Move over."

Jaylin quickly sat up. I wondered if he still had on his black silk pajama pants or if he was naked. I couldn't see because the sheets covered him. "Are you out of your gotdamn mind? You'd better get away from this bed, Jada, before you get hurt."

"Ooo, hurt me, baby," I said, snatching his cover off and hopping on his bed. He snatched the cover away from me and stood up.

"Stop playing, all right? I'm tired, baby, and the last thing you want to do is interrupt my sleep. Get back over there in your bed and go to sleep."

"Nope. If you're tired, then I suggest you lay down. I'll hold you so you can go back to sleep. Just don't bring that dick of yours anywhere near me; I'm not ready for my head to be all fucked up. I bet you have bitches walkin' around like zombies, don't you?"

Jaylin gave me an intense stare and then walked away to go get in my bed. That was when I saw he still had on his pajama pants. I followed and got in my bed with him. "You about to get cussed the hell out!" he shouted. "You got some mental shit going on that you need to take care of soon!"

He walked back to the other bed and so did I. After he got in the bed, I followed suit. We were back-to-back with each other and there was little room in the bed. We both were near the edge. I let out a deep breath and crossed my leg over his. He said not one word, until I let out a silent fart that seeped out and blew his way. Responding quickly to my bad manners, he picked up the fluffy pillow and hit me hard in my face with it. Hit me so hard, my face stung.

"So, you doin' it like that?" My mouth was wide open. "Really?"

I tried to hit him with my pillow, but he ducked. "That was foul, Jada," he said, shaking his head. "You got this whole room smelling like a rotten-ass egg!"

"Fuck!" Prince shouted and threw his cover aside. "Nigga can't get no sleep up in here. Why don't you motherfuckers go to sleep?"

"Why don't you shut the hell up and pretend that you don't hear us?" I fired back.

Next thing I knew, Prince threw something like a flying saucer and it hit me in the back. When it hit the floor, I thought it was a shoe.

"Now what you got to say about that, stupid bitch? Go check yo drawers because they stankin'."

Maybe they were stankin', but I wasn't about to let him get away with calling me no bitch and throwing things at me. He needed to know that I didn't get down like that, no siree. I wasted no time rushing over to him, fist-first. The lights came on, and, by that time, I had got in one punch to Prince's head. Roc was out of bed holding Prince back. Jaylin held me, but I struggled to get away from him. No luck.

"Man, let that bitch go so she can walk straight into my fist!" Prince hollered out. "I'm tryin' to snooze and she up playin' night games and shit!"

"You mad 'cause I'm not playin' them with you? Is that what it is? Nobody else complainin', but you."

Chase cleared her throat. "I wasn't complaining, but it does stink in here. Your voice was keeping me up, too. I understand where Prince is coming from."

I'd just about had it with this heifer. She was jealous, too, especially since Jaylin hadn't given her no attention. I snatched away from him, pretending as if everything was all-good. Roc released Prince, and nearly five minutes later, they got back in their beds.

"I hope we can all get some sleep now," Sylvia said, yawning. "Somebody please turn off the light."

"I got it," I said, going close by the door to hit the light switch. Once they were out, I walked by Chase's bed and hurled one of Roc's tennis shoes at her head, in hopes that it knocked some sense into her.

"Ouch!" she yelled. "Who threw that? Jada?"

I definitely wasn't backing down. "And what if I did?"

I could see a shadow of her coming my way, so I reached for her ponytail in the dark, pulling, twisting, turning it and trying to break her damn neck. This bitch and I went at it, and we were swinging wildly at each other. She got off a few good punches, but I backed her up to the bed and crawled on top of her. The lights came on and she did her best to roll on top of me. She pulled my hair, yanking it so hard that we fell on the floor, where I dragged her across it and punched at her face. She kept kicking her legs and swinging, while trying to get in as many punches as possible.

"Let my damn hair go!" she shouted and rolled on her knees to avoid my punches to her face. That allowed me to pound the back of her head.

"This is what happens to bitches who cross me! Let this ass kickin' serve as a lesson!"

"Stop this madness," Sylvia said, but was nowhere near us. "This crap is embarrassing."

Jaylin and Roc took their time breaking us apart from each other. Probably because Chase's negligee had ripped and she was damn near naked. Prince was all smiles and he chanted "get her ass" the whole time. I was sure he was rooting for Chase.

Finally, Roc held Chase back by her waist and she loved every bit of it. "That's what you get, tramp," she said, touching her lip. Yeah, it was bleeding and I had a handful of her weave in my hand.

I could barely catch my breath. Jaylin stood in front of me with his arms folded and as I tried to go around him, he pushed me back. I continued to charge toward Chase. "You didn't do nothin', did you? All you did was show yo ass, which Roc already done been up in that!" I shouted.

"Whatever, Jada," she said. "Just so you know, I will fight your fat ass anytime, any day and anywhere. Don't think I'm no punk."

"This is ridiculous," Sylvia griped. "I'm never going to get any sleep."

She left the room and Prince got up, too. "I could stand a cup of coffee or somethin'. Let me know when y'all get done in here."

Chase asked Roc to let her go, and when he did, she went into the closet. Hopefully to change clothes; the negligee she had on was nothing but shreds.

Jaylin and Roc looked at each other with smirks on their faces, but at the same time, shaking their heads. I didn't give a shit, but I hoped that I sent a message to everybody in here—mess with me and you will get your ass whooped.

Sylvia

I wasn't sure if I could go another day in this house. I was tired as ever, and after what had happened between Jaylin and me, I couldn't even look at him. Part of me was embarrassed by the entire thing. Then again, I was ashamed. I still wanted a piece of the action; even after knowing he was a good friend of Jonathan's. Pertaining to him, I seriously could not shake that man for nothing in the world. And I often found myself daydreaming about our numerous sexual escapades, in particular, one that happened in the office copy room. It was the first time we'd hooked up and it definitely wasn't the last.

Nearly everyone in the office had left that day, but as usual, I hung around to see what else I could get off my plate. I didn't mind working overtime; I was deeply in love with my boss. As his Administrative Assistant, I wanted everything to be in order. I was in the copy room making copies of several spreadsheets Jonathan needed for his meeting tomorrow. Piles of paper were stacked everywhere, and the copy machine was so loud that I couldn't hear a thing. My gray, short fuzzy skirt gripped every bit of my big butt, as well as my hips that I often swayed from side to side to get Jonathan's attention. My black silk blouse revealed a healthy part of my cleavage and my black stilettos increased my height by five inches.

With my back facing the door, I glanced at the round clock on the wall, seeing that it was already ten minutes to six. I had hoped to be done by six-thirty, so I could get home and check out my favorite TV show. The room was kind of stuffy, and when I realized that a few beads of sweat had dotted my forehead, I reached over to the thermostat to lower the temperature. As soon as my hand touched the thermostat, I felt another set of hands on my hips. I was startled, but then again, I already knew who was behind me from the smell of his intoxicating cologne that always left me breathless. I was shocked that he had touched me in such a way, but without saying a word, I reached my hand up to rub the back of his head.

"I need you, Sylvia," Jonathan whispered with his lips close to my ear. "I need you now."

Without hesitating, I said three words to my best friend's husband. "Take me now."

He slowly undid the buttons on my silk blouse, one by one. He then pulled it open, massaging my breasts together and manipulating my hard nipples. I squirmed from the feel of his hands touching me, and unable to stop this, I turned around to face him. We stared into each other's eyes, knowing that what we were about to do was wrong on so many different levels. Jonathan, however, inched my mini skirt over the curve of my hips and eased my lace panties down. I happily stepped out of them and then turned to face the copier. I bent slightly over, and displaying how flexible I was, I hiked my right leg on top of the copier so that Jonathan could have easier access to my pussy. He held my leg in place with one hand and unzipped his pants with the other. They dropped to his ankles, and it didn't take long for him to step out of his pants and shoes. He pressed his hardness against my butt, but that was only to tease me. I remained quiet as ever, but I held my breath when Jonathan dropped to his knees and began to take light licks between my legs. My pussy was staring him right in the face, and enjoying every bit of his delicate licks, his tongue searched deeper and hit a hot spot that caused my legs to buckle.

"Hold on, baby," he said. "I need to taste a bit more of this."

I closed my eyes and tried to focus elsewhere, but couldn't. Jonathan's thick fingers kept circling my clit, and after two more minutes of his outstanding pussy-licking performance, I was ready to spray his face with my juices. He, however, stopped in mid-action and returned to standing behind me. He aimed the chunky meat on his head right at my sopping wet slit and teased the hell out of me by rubbing it against my walls. Seconds later, he inched his way in, causing me to halt my breathing again. I squeezed my eyes, thinking that my best friend's husband's dick felt even better than I ever imagined it would. The feel was so spectacular that I bounced my ass against him to bring more pleasure. The sounds of my gushing pussy juices echoed in the tiny room, and Jonathan could hear, see and feel how excited I was to receive all that he was giving me.

"This pussy is so wet and good, baby, that I can barely stand. I want this shit to last longer; let's move over to the chair or table," he suggested.

I hated for him to pull out of me, but when he chose to sit in the chair, I straddled him and positioned his dick to enter me again. This time, I moved at a slow pace that caused him to drop his head back and close his eyes in thought. Jonathan held my ass and pulled my cheeks far apart so his thick meat could sink further into me. We both moaned together, giving the chair a real workout. It squeaked, rolled around, and almost tilted over as I gave Jonathan the best ride that I could possibly give him. It was so obvious that in this moment, and at this time, neither of us had any regrets. None, but it didn't mean that I couldn't tell that Jonathan had something heavy on his mind. The way he kept shaking his head said so, and when he lowered his head to suck my breasts, I held his face with my hands, lifting it. I sucked his thick lips with mine and then stared into his serious, pain-filled eyes. I could now see the hurt in them and had started to regret my aggressiveness. A slow tear rolled down my cheek, but I continued to ride him.

"I had to do this, Jonathan," I said tearfully. "Please don't hate me for betraying Dana."

Jonathan said not one word. He rose from the chair, securing me in his strong arms. Afterward, he laid me on the floor and maneuvered his body in between my legs. I wrapped my healthy legs around him and he rubbed up and down them before entering my wetness again. He then searched into my eyes, looking for answers about his wife who was cheating on him with a much younger man.

"I've had a rough day, Sylvia. I'm hurting and I know you have the answers for me. Please, tell me. I'm begging you to tell me if Dana is cheating on me. If so, I need to know with who?" He dropped his head on my chest, but before he did, I could see his eyes fill with water.

At that point, I wasn't sure why we were doing this. It seemed as if Jonathan was using me and trying to get answers about his wife. She'd been cheating on him for a very long time, and it angered me that she could have a man as gentle and kind as Jonathan, yet not appreciate him. So confused, I pressed my hand against Jonathan's chest for him to back away from me. His limp dick slid out of me, but I could feel a flood of my juices raining down my crack. I sat up on my elbows, looking at him and not knowing what to say.

"Jonathan, I told you before that—"

"Please!" he yelled and then slumped his head again. The loud pitch of his voice caused my eyes to widen and he demanded to know the truth. "It's Lewis, isn't it? Just tell me, damn it! Is it Lewis?"

Refusing to answer, I quickly stood up and pulled down my skirt. Jonathan rushed up from the floor and reached out to embrace me. This was such a horrible situation to be in and he could see that I was about to lose it. No matter what, though, he continued to beg for answers.

"I'm begging you, Sylvia, please." He continued to hold my trembling body. "Just tell me if it's Lewis. That's all I need is a yes or no."

My dry mouth finally opened. I could barely speak. Jonathan did need *to know the truth. I wasn't so sure if I was willing to tell it because I knew what Dana had done to him was wrong or because I wanted him for myself. Either way, I whispered "yes" and told him that Dana had been cheating with Lewis for the past three years.*

That day, Jonathan left the office distraught and he put a plan together to end his marriage. There was no doubt that I had been a key participant in the backstabbing mess before and here I was playing the same game again. I promised myself that I would never go there again. Jonathan had no idea I was in this house with Jaylin, but what if they talked and Jaylin told him how desperate I came across? This was hard. I didn't know if I could get through the next three months without finding myself in a situation like I did with him last night. Or maybe he was too drunk to remember anything. He had been drinking, so I kept my fingers crossed, hoping that he wouldn't be able to recall much about our encounter.

It was seven o'clock in the morning. The only person still asleep was Chase. Actually, I wasn't sure if she was sleep or not. Maybe pretending to be sleep because she was too embarrassed to show her face after getting her tail beat by Jada. That was a complete mess. I was upset with Jada, too, and I heard her messing around with Jaylin all night. I was glad that he'd told me that she wasn't his type. And it was good to know that I was.

Jada was in the kitchen with a scarf tied around her head, looking like Aunt Jemima. Mary J's "No More Drama" was blasting through the speakers and Jada was singing the lyrics as she cooked. She was whipping up pancake batter and had eggs, bacon, sausage and hash browns on the counter. It looked as if she was ready to throw down, so I asked if she needed some help while I prepared my coffee.

"No, I got this," she said. "Since I messed up everybody's sleep, I'm fixin' a good breakfast this mornin'."

"I'm sure everyone will appreciate that. Where are the fellas at anyway?"

"Did you have to ask? You know they're in that workout room, tryin' to keep those bodies lookin' good."

"Yes, I should have known."

Still in my pajamas, I reached for the newspaper on the counter and headed outside to read the paper and drink my coffee. From a distance, I could see Roc, Jaylin and Prince in the workout room. Good for them, I thought. I intended to do some aerobics later on to keep myself in shape.

I sat at a round table with an umbrella. As I started to read the paper, Chase came outside looking beat. She had on a pink silk robe, and I couldn't believe it when I saw a bruise underneath her eye. Did Jada do it like that? Maybe I missed it; after all, they had also been fighting in the dark. Chase sat next to me with orange juice filled to the rim of her glass.

"Morning," she said with a somber look washed across her face.

"Good morning. Are you okay?"

"I'm absolutely fine. A little tired, but I'm going to take a long nap around noon."

"That's good. I'm tired, too. Stayed up real late last night and I couldn't get back to sleep, especially after that fight with you and Jada."

"Sorry about that," she said. "But she came at me first. I was unprepared for what happened, but next time I won't be."

"Why does there have to be a next time? Just ignore her, Chase. We women don't need to be conducting ourselves like that. You come across to me as a real lady who doesn't get down like that," I lied. Chase was just as hood as Jada. She faked the looks of a classy woman, but it most certainly did not apply.

"I am a respectful woman, but I can be pushed to react. I'm

going to do my best to ignore Jada, especially to keep down confusion. So, on another note, how did it go with Jaylin last night? Was he everything that you thought he would be?"

I glanced over Chase's shoulder, seeing the men heading our way. Sweat definitely does a body good, no doubt. Hanging basketball shorts were a plus and since neither of them had on shirts, my eyes didn't know where to look. "I guess he was everything I needed him to be," I said to Chase. "But we'll talk later."

Chase turned around, giving it away that I had said something about the men. I saw her lick her lips and then turn back around. Roc was the first one to take a seat, but Jaylin stood next to me, reaching for the newspaper. The smooth, minimal hair above his shaft would make any woman want to drop to her knees and take him all in. He was putting it out there, and boy, was he sexy. If those shorts slid down one or two more inches, Chase would faint.

Prince threw a towel over his shoulder and looked at Chase. "Damn, ma, you got fucked up. I was rootin' for you, but next time you go toe-to-toe with a big bitch like that, trip her. That's the only way you'll win." Chase cut her eyes at Prince and he looked at Roc. "Time for me to take a hot shower. In a minute, man, I'll holla."

Roc tossed his head back and Prince walked away. Roc picked up Chase's orange juice while Jaylin took a seat next to me. I was nervous.

"Why are you drinking up all of my orange juice?" Chase said, as Roc guzzled it down.

"Because I'm thirsty. I really need a cold glass of ice water, but I'm too tired to go get it."

"In other words, you want me to go get it? And if I do, remember that you must give a little to get a whole lot in return." She winked and stood up.

Roc smiled and watched as she went inside to get his water. "I plan to give a whole lot!" he shouted out to her. "But patience, ma, patience!"

Chase smiled and appeared to be in a better mood. Roc, however, looked at Jaylin, who was reading the financial section of the newspaper.

"Breakfast smellin' like Goody Goody on Natural Bridge," Roc said. "I can't wait another minute to eat. You comin' inside to eat or are you gon' wait on Jada to bring it out here to you? I'm goin' inside, just in case she and Chase start cat-fighting again."

Jaylin shrugged his shoulders. "Let me know if they do, so I can watch. Meanwhile, tell Jada I said hurry it up with my food. I want some V8 juice, too, and grits if she has any."

Apparently, Jaylin and Roc enjoyed watching the fight, or more like it, they enjoyed seeing Chase near naked. Personally, I thought it was a darn shame, but I kept my mouth shut.

Roc went inside and Jaylin and I sat in silence for a while. I sipped my coffee, then started to bite my nails.

"Why are you nervous?" Jaylin questioned with his eyes still focused on the paper.

"I'm not."

"Yes, you are."

"Okay, just a little. Only because of what happened last night."

He put the paper down. "I told you not to worry about it. What happened in that bathroom last night is between you and me. How pretty that ass is and the heat coming from that pussy stays in my mind, no one else."

My eyes widened from his bluntness. "Okay. But did you have to say it like that?"

"It's not any different from you telling me your pussy was tingling. 'Make it stop, Jaylin, please make it stop.' Remember?"

I covered my mouth in shame. "Yes, I do, but I regret that you do, too."

"Kind of hard to forget. You feel me?"

Every single inch of him, I wanted to say, but I took a hard swallow instead. I ran my fingers through my braids and then sat up straight as I felt myself slumped in my seat. When I looked up, Jada was rushing outside with a plate in her hand. It was boiling over with stacks of bacon, sausage and pancakes that were leaning to the side. With glee in her eyes, she put the plate in front of Jaylin. It also had a mountain of cheese eggs and grits to go with it.

"Here you go, Boo-Boo," she said with a wide smile. She pinched his cheek, but he smacked her hand away from it. "This is for me interruptin' your sleep last night. I'll try my best not to let it happen again."

Jaylin stared at the plate in awe. "If this is breakfast, let me guess what's for dinner. Fatback ribs and pork-n-beans with ham hocks. Are you serious? Do you really expect for me to eat all of this shit?"

She twirled her fingers through the curls in his hair. "Every last bit of it, baby, but don't yo ass be ungrateful now, okay? It looks like your food only goes to one place anyway, and even if that gets fatter, I doubt that you will hear any complaints."

"I'm satisfied with the size of that already, so I suggest that you try this again. Bring me a fruit salad and some wheat toast. Spread a little jelly on it and don't forget the V8."

Jada backed away from him and folded her arms. "See what happens when you try to be nice to these niggas? They take advantage of the shit. Neva satisfied with nothin', and how dare you think you can give me orders and that I'm supposed to run like Mighty Joe Young and cater to you? I haven't had none of yo dick yet, so I'm not bowin' down to you. Sylvia may do it, but fasho not me."

Jaylin had heard enough. He stood and picked up the plate from the table. "And see what happens when a non-following-directions trick don't want to listen? Chill out with that nigga bullshit or else."

He dumped the entire plate in the trashcan and went inside. Jada followed after him, ranting about what he'd done and said to her.

"Chase!" Jaylin yelled, trying to irritate Jada as they went inside. "Come get her, would you?"

I shook my head, but remained outside, in thought about what had transpired last night. Who knew if anything would revolve from it? I didn't know, but after my conversation with Jaylin, I suspected that my feelings for Jonathan, or Jaylin's friendship with him, would come to a head.

Prince

The silly tricks in this house were constantly at each other's throats and that was a good thing. Eventually, they'd get tired of the back-and-forth bickering and leave in anger. That was the plan we had, and Roc and Jaylin were with me on this.

What they didn't know was I had been working on them behind the scenes as well. Roc was cool, but last night, I remembered some shit about a beef I had with his Uncle Ronnie. That nigga was now six-feet under, but he used to be cool with my sperm donor. And anybody who was down with that fool couldn't be on my team. Not even his nephew the streets knew as Roc.

As for Jaylin, he was too busy trying to look good. I had already peeped his shit in the closet, figuring that he had some serious paper. Paper that I considered lining my pockets with, even though I'd have some when I won this challenge. I suspected he had some dollars on him, but after searching through his pockets, I came up empty-handed.

I did, however, find a whack note from his woman, encouraging him not to stay away for long, telling him how much she loved him and asking for forgiveness so they could move on in a positive way for the sake of their children. His daughter wrote something, too, but I didn't really read that bullshit. All I saw was her hand-print and a smiley face. No wonder he seemed on edge. I had a lack of respect for men who allowed women to have them uptight and that nigga was real uptight.

So, while all these fools had their minds on sex, panties were hitting the floor and asses in the air, I intended to make my move. I wanted everybody on my good side, even Jada who I intended to apologize to later. In no way would it be a sincere apology, but I had to pretend as if everything was sweet. That was how I got over on people to get ahead. Befriend them and then move in for the kill.

I sat on one of the beanbag chairs in the living room watching *SpongeBob Squarepants*. It was what Jada wanted to watch, and I wasn't about to argue with her, even though I wasn't interested in watching this silly shit. Roc sat on a stool in the kitchen with his Beats by Dre headphones on. A blue bandana was tied around his head, holding his waves intact. "Shake that booty meat," he kept repeating like the song did and was tapping his hands on the counter. He seemed to be in his own world, while Chase was in the bedroom with Jaylin. I assumed Sylvia was in the workout area because I hadn't seen her come inside yet.

"Breakfast was off the chain, ma," I said, attempting to make peace with Jada. "Where you learn to cook like that at?"

"My grandmother," she said and then belched from taking a swallow from a tall glass of Kool-Aid that sat on the table in front of her. "Oh, excuse me. But my grandmother used to throw down and she taught me how to cook, since that crack-head mama of mine wasn't around to do it."

"Give big ups to yo grandmother for me then, all right? And I feel you on that mama thing 'cause mine had her hang ups, too."

Jada smiled, and after eating two fistfuls of Cheetos from her hands, she lifted her feet on the table so she could polish her toenails. "My grandmother restin' peacefully in her grave, boy, but

I know she hears you. You need to wait until dinner. I'm gon' barbecue some ribs, hot dogs, whoop, whoop, whoop and make some fire potato salad. My sauce be off the chain."

"Can't wait. I bet it do."

Jada got back to polishing her toenails, and now that we were on good terms again, I went into the kitchen with Roc. He bobbed his head to the music and pointed to Jada.

"Is that you?" he whispered.

I shook my head, implying no, since he couldn't hear me. Fuck nah, that gutter bitch wasn't me. "Me" was at her grandmother's house, waiting for her Prince to safely return home. I loved me some Poetry Wright and there wasn't a chick in the world that would ever come between us.

Roc removed the headphones and laid them on the table. We looked in another direction when we saw Jaylin swoop around the corner, looking like he had a beef with somebody.

"I need to have a talk with everybody in this house," he said with creases in his forehead.

"What up?" Roc questioned.

Jaylin didn't respond. He went to get Sylvia from the workout area and asked Chase to come out of the bedroom. She did and we all stood around to hear what his gripe was.

"First of all," he said. "I hung my things in the closet away from everybody else, in hopes that no one would touch my shit. When I go in there today, I noticed that two of my pants pockets were pulled out, a letter is missing and somebody sprayed some of my cologne. Within the hour, I want that letter in my hands, and I want to know who is responsible for going through my things. If I do not find out who is responsible, well, I can show you better than I can tell you."

All of the ladies' eyes shifted to me, but Roc spoke up first.

"On a for real tip, you need to tone down that noise and those threats. I don't take them lightly and ain't no need to get all swoll over a missin' letter and some cologne. You don't know for sure if somebody went through your pockets. With cameras all around, I can't see nobody bein' that stupid where they would ramble through yo shit."

The creases in Jaylin's forehead deepened. The look on his face implied that he didn't approve of Roc's response. That was good news for me.

"You can take that tip and shove it up your ass. I don't give a fuck how you feel about my threats. The one I made will be certified and delivered. Cameras or not, *you* or some other nosey muthafucka ventured where you shouldn't have. Fess up or else."

Everybody looked at Roc, waiting for him to respond. I knew he was capable of knocking pretty boy the hell out; I was waiting on him to do it. Roc stepped up to Jaylin, leaving no breathing room in between them.

"Talk is cheap, so I'm not gon' spend a lot of time up in here runnin' my mouth. If you believe that I went through yo shit, let's step the fuck outside so we can settle this once and for all."

Roc stormed away, removing his wife-beater and going outside. My money was on him. Jaylin wasted no time following him, but he stopped when Sylvia grabbed his arm.

"No, Jaylin," she said. "I...I was the one who looked through your things, not Roc or anyone else in here."

Why did she lie like that? She knew damn well she wasn't the one because I was. Jaylin stopped at the sliding doors. His eyes were without a blink. "You? Where is my fucking letter at?"

"I tore it up and threw it in the trashcan. I apologize, and please don't be upset—"

His face was twisted with much anger as he went into the kitchen and searched through the trash. "Where the hell is it?" he shouted. "Get over here and find it!"

Sylvia looked nervous as hell. Everybody stood still, trying to see what would ultimately happen. Roc came back inside and even he was still fuming.

"I'm waitin', muthafucka." He held out his hands. "What's takin' you so long, punk?"

"Sylvia's nosey-ass self went through his stuff," Jada said to Roc. "Calm down and breathe a little, baby; you're sweatin' too much. I hate to see you lookin' like a madman and that look ain't gon' do you no good, if you get yo ass beat. I'm just sayin'."

"Shut the fuck up talkin' to me," Roc said to Jada. "And ain't nobody gon' beat my ass—you can be sure of that."

Jada's neck started to roll, but before any words left her mouth, Jaylin responded to Roc.

"I wouldn't be so confident if I were you. And when I get done with this, I'mma show you who the real punk is. That way you won't have any doubts."

"Stop all of this, okay?" Sylvia said, giving Jaylin the torn letter. "I said I'm sorry and I won't touch your things again. You can now apologize to Roc for accusing him, and Roc, you can apologize to Jaylin for not believing him. No need to fight about something that was my fault to begin with."

Jaylin shot her a look that could kill, snatched the torn paper from her hand and walked off. Roc eyeballed him and then went back outside. I was confused as hell because I knew damn well that Sylvia didn't throw the letter in the trashcan. Something was up; I could feel it.

"Ole trouble-making hussy," Jada whispered underneath her breath, referring to Sylvia. Jada went outside to where Roc was and demanded an apology from him. I wasn't sure if she would get it or not, but it was in her best interest to pull the fuck back and go sit her ass down somewhere. Chase returned to the bedroom, leaving Sylvia and me in the kitchen.

She glared at me with a strange look in her eyes. As I started to walk away, she grabbed my arm. "Watch yourself, Prince. Just so you know, I'm keeping my eyes on you."

I shrugged. "So what? Am I supposed to be afraid or somethin'?"

"Yeah, you should be, especially if you don't want to be arrested for stealing."

"Ain't a damn thing up in here I want, and just as an FYI, I was only searchin' through Jaylin's shit to check him out. You didn't witness me take anything from him, so why you around here actin' like I'm a kleptomaniac?"

"Because you are."

This bitch didn't know me, and I hated for people to judge me based on my looks, especially black people who fell in line with stereotypes that destroyed us all. I stepped closer to Sylvia, very unappreciative of the noise she was bringing. "Why are you so sure of yourself? Is it because I fit the bill of a young black man who don't do nothin' in life but take from people of his own race, right? I have a problem with people like you who play into that bullshit 'cause in reality, you don't know shit. So the next time you think about coverin' for me, don't. I can handle myself and there is a reason behind every single thing I do."

Sylvia didn't back away from me, but her brows were raised and anger was deep within her eyes. "All you should be doing right now is thanking me for sparing you a butt kicking you were about to get from a man who, obviously, values his possessions. So much so that he'll kill for them. I don't know what he has that interests you, and it makes no sense that you would be curious about a man who is nowhere near your level."

"You don't appear to be on that level either, but that hasn't stopped you from showin' interest in his dick. I don't get why any of this is yo business, and you really need to take your nosey ass somewhere and chill. Bein' up in mine will get you nowhere, but it may get you kicked out of this house or possibly kicked in yo ass. I don't know which one you prefer, but how about you tell me?"

"How about I don't have time to entertain clueless, young idiots like you who refuse to listen? Just stay out of other people's stuff and we won't have this problem again."

Sylvia walked away in one direction, and I kept it moving in another. I stood on the patio with my thoughts locked on what I had to do to get her nosey ass out of here. I considered her a thorn in my side, and the last thing I needed was somebody looking over their shoulder, watching me.

Roc

That shit with Jaylin shook me up earlier. I was still hot about it. He's lucky that Sylvia opened her mouth because had he came outside, that would've been it for his ass. Who in the hell did he think he was, talking to me like I was some kind of flunky or something? Many niggas were put six-feet under for bringin' heat like that, and it was only because of Desa Rae that I learned to calm myself in situations like that one. If we were on my turf, I wasn't so sure if it would've gone down like that. That nigga would be somewhere leaking for sure.

Things had settled down some, and Jada was outside grilling some hamburgers, ribs and hotdogs. There was no question that she loved to cook, but this was too much damn food. The next person on the cooking schedule was me, so I figured everybody better enjoy themselves because I wasn't going to cook much. And if I did, nine times out of ten, I'd probably be serving burnt food.

Trying to let out my frustrations, I started to hoop with Prince. Chase was messing around near the pool area and Jada was doing her thing with the grill. Sylvia was probably somewhere kissing Jaylin's ass. He had been swoll all day about what had happened, but he couldn't even find the words to at least apologize. Not that I would accept his apology; I didn't squash beefs that easily. I held grudges and this incident left a bad taste in my mouth.

"Some shit you gotta let roll off yo back and not sweat it," Prince said as he tossed the basketball at my chest. It bounced off and hit the ground. I grabbed the ball and gripped it with both hands. I looked at the hoop, trying to decide if I should take the long shot. It was near three-point range, so I tucked the ball underneath my arm and vented some more.

"I find it hard to believe that nigga got at me like he didn't have no sense. I don't know where he from, where he think people supposed to be afraid when he speak or they supposed to run when he say run. Don't he know that everything about me shows that I don't get down like that?"

Prince tried to smack the ball from my hand, so I dribbled a little, took the shot and missed. We rushed to get the ball, but he got it before I did. As he dribbled the ball, he replied to my comment.

"I noticed that shit about him five minutes after I walked into this house. I don't know what's the deal with that nigga either, but you and me need to put our heads together to come up with something to get him out of here. He seems like a smart man, and aside from the bitches in here, he's the one who I really think can win this challenge."

Prince shot the ball and made it. He tightened his fist and smiled at me. "Get yo mind right or you about to lose this game," he said.

He was right, and more than anything, I hated to lose. But as he passed the ball to me, I was in thought about what he'd said.

"I don't think a plan is required to get that fool out of here because today he showed he was weak. All he need is a good ass kickin' that may bring him back to reality. Sometimes, that's all it takes and he got one more time to trip like he did today. After that, it's all over with for that fool."

I dribbled the ball down the court and then took my shot and made it. The game was getting real deep between us, so I dropped my thoughts about that punk Jaylin and made a comeback when I beat Prince. Afterward, I sat at one of the tables by the pool, thinking about Miss Desa Rae Jenkins. That was when I heard Chase call my name.

"What?" I replied.

"Stop frowning and get in the water so we can have some fun."

"I'm not feelin' that right now, but I enjoy watchin' you."

She smiled and swam away. I felt bad for Chase because on a for real tip, Jada beat that ass last night. She drug Chase around like a ragdoll, but my eyes were glued on the goodies. Chase's body was sweet. I actually dreamed about fucking her last night, but all the bullshit that was happening today had my mind elsewhere.

"I guess I don't have to ask why you're so quiet today, do I?" Jada said, sitting next to me. She had on a yellow sundress that made her look twice her size. I appreciated her thickness, but her attitude was too much for me.

"I'm just chillin', ma. Tryin' to steer clear from trouble, so I don't have to get into nobody's shit like you did last night."

"I couldn't help myself. Chase was askin' for it and she kept pokin' her nose where it didn't belong. You ain't mad at me, are you?"

"Why would I be mad at you?"

"Because Chase your girl, ain't she? And you haven't said much to me since I've been in this house."

"That's because I got some heavy shit on my mind. And just so you know, Chase ain't my girl. I barely know anything about her."

"Don't matter. You did have sex with her yesterday, didn't you?"

"That's what you're assumin'. If you think we got down like that, that's on you."

"Well, you ain't denyin' it."

"I don't have to. It really ain't yo business, is it?"

Jada got quiet. She blew a big bubble with the gum she had in her mouth and then chewed. "I'm not tryin' to get all up in yo business or anything, Roc, but you'd better watch Chase. She real sneaky and I know her kind. You seem like a cool person and you really remind me of a dude I used to date named Kiley."

"Oh, yeah. How's that?"

"Y'all got that swag, if you know what I mean. I love those dimples and he was almost your skin color, too. He was the head nigga in charge and couldn't nobody tell him nothin'. I miss him so much, and when I saw you, it took me back to our relationship."

"I take it y'all ain't together no more. What happened?"

"I tripped. Let some other bitch get her hands on him. After that, there was no turnin' back for him."

"It be like that sometimes, ma, but what's for you is for you. What's not will never be."

"I agree. But I'm glad to be here. I hope you and me can get closer through all of this."

"One day at a time. Ain't no tellin' what will happen here."

Jada agreed and got up. I followed and got me a hot dog bun to get a hot dog. I piled it high with potato salad and with some of her special sauce. When I bit into it, I could have died. That shit was good; so sick that I had to lick around my lips.

"Damn, girl, you be puttin' your foot in yo food. What the hell is in that sauce?"

Jada laughed and bumped her hip with mine. "A little bit of this and that and a whole lot of sweetness, baby. Put one right here," she said, pointing to her cheek. "Show me how much you appreciate a good cook, and that you forgive me for earlier pokin' my nose where it didn't belong."

"I forgive you. Just don't let it happen again, all right?"

Jada didn't reply, but I knew she understood what I'd said. I licked more sauce from my lips and smacked them together. I pecked Jada on her lips, catching her off guard. Her eyes bugged and she was all smiles. "Don't get hurt up in here, Roc. You need to stop playin', bay-be; please quit while you're ahead."

I laughed at Jada and then went inside so I could get a plate. Prince had gone inside and was now playing videogames. Jaylin was sitting at the computer desk. I grabbed a paper plate from the counter, but when Jaylin came into the kitchen, I put it down, in case he still had *issues*. He leaned against the counter and stroked his trimmed goatee.

"Look, I got at you the incorrect way earlier," he said. "Had I known Sylvia was the one fucking with my things, I would've addressed her, instead of everybody else."

"I'm sure you would've, but was that an apology you swingin' my way?"

"I apologize to no one, so you can either take what I said or leave it. It doesn't matter to me either way. I've done my part and I will do no more."

"I'm gon' do my part, too. I should've believed what you said, but what you said didn't matter to me because I don't care about the next man's property. With that, this shit is a wrap."

I left the kitchen to go back outside and get something to eat. Ten minutes later, Jaylin came outside and Prince followed a little later. The fellas sat at one table eating and the ladies were at another.

"Don't choke yourself over there, Jaylin." Jada giggled, as she caught him licking the sauce off his fingers. "You look like you're enjoyin' the food."

"Not really. I'm pretending that it's something else to eat like your pussy."

We laughed, but the ladies shook their heads. "You a foul-mouth dirty, nasty nig…fool that really needs to quit," Jada said. "I want my props. If you don't give them to me, I'm gon' keep you up at night again."

"I promise that you will find yourself on the floor tonight if I don't get any sleep. What went down last night will not happen again."

"If I'm on the floor, so are you. So stop tryin' to chasertise me for keepin' you up. The only reason you were up was because you were in that bathroom gettin' it in."

"Chastise, Jada," Chase said, correcting her again. "You can get mad at me all you want to, but I'm only trying to help you by pointing out your incorrect grammar."

Jada narrowed her eyes and glared at Chase without a blink.

"Close the piano and turn out the lights," Prince said, laughing. "Pack it up because this party is over!"

Chase continued. "Party over or not, Jada needs to appreciate me for speaking up about it. Nobody else is willing to say anything, and it's a shame when we allow *our* people to speak this way around us and not say one word. She may not thank me now, but she'll be thanking me later."

Prince grabbed his plate off the table and rushed toward the house. "I'm out. When fists start flyin', and blood start sheddin', I don't want to be nowhere around."

I wasn't about to let Jada and Chase get down again, even though it gave me a rise to see some nakedness. Since they were chilling at the same table, I thought everything was all-good. I guessed not.

Sylvia spoke up, somewhat agreeing with Chase. "I get what Chase is trying to say, Jada, but it may be coming across the wrong way. Instead of embarrassing you in front of everybody, maybe

Chase should think about pulling you aside and telling you about her concerns when the two of you are alone."

"If you think that's the appropriate way to do it, Sylvia, then why haven't you done it?" Chase said with snap in her voice. "I hate people who sit back and never say anything, until somebody else does."

"It was a suggestion, Chase. And I'm not going to sit here and argue with you over something so ridiculous."

Jada slammed her hand on the table and crumbled up a piece of newspaper. She formed it into a ball and held it in her hand.

"I am so sick and tired of tryin' to be nice to people. Both of you bitches really need to get a life and mind your own business. How many times do I have to say not to correct me? Don't worry about my grammar, hoes! Focus elsewhere and continue to chase dick like the two of you are doin' so well. I haven't said one word about that, even though desperate women irk the hell out of me."

Jada threw the wad of paper at Chase's face, got up from the table and bolted toward the house. She slid the door aside, almost cracking the glass from slamming it so hard. All Chase did was yell that she had something for her later, but I was sure it wouldn't be her fist because those weren't capable of causing Jada much harm. I happened to look at Jaylin who was leaned back in the chair, resting his index finger along the side of his face. If I didn't know any better, I'd think he was smiling. He was, and deep down, so was I.

Chase

I wasn't going to sugarcoat anything or beat around the bush. Jada did get the best of me last night and I was fuming inside, as I waited on the opportunity to get revenge. There was no way for me to let something like that go; walking around here with a black-eye was pretty embarrassing. Roc seemed to give me a little sympathy, but Jaylin still hadn't said much to me.

At this point, I really didn't care much about this challenge. I wasn't trying to be the last person standing. All I wanted was revenge and a piece of Roc. His rejecting me made me want him even more. I surely thought getting at him would be much easier, but I was wrong. It was one thing after another and it seemed as if he wasn't with it.

Tonight, I would push harder, to see if I could get us back on the right track. Maybe I could persuade Jaylin, too, but when I saw him kissing Sylvia in the pool, I was through with him. Then, he got in her shit this morning, and from the way he cussed at her, I assumed he was done. Good for him because her actions were way out of line. What kind of woman went through a man's things that she didn't know? What did she expect to learn or gain from going through his stuff? That was a very immature move and she should be embarrassed for coming off as a psycho woman with issues.

I spent most of the day cleaning this house. It was my way of staying away from Jada and not correcting her when she said the wrong thing. I really saw it as me doing her a favor and to hell with her if she thought otherwise. I didn't like her attitude, and I didn't like the way she kept playing around with Jaylin. I kept asking myself if something was there between the two of them because they really seemed chummy around here. There were times when I saw him checking her out, and she couldn't keep his name out of her mouth. I could never imagine him being with a woman like her, and I had to keep the faith that she was on a very different level than he was.

I threw the dirty rag in a bucket and pulled off the rubber gloves to wash my hands. The bathroom wasn't as filthy as I thought it would be, but with so many people using the shower, it had to be cleaned every day. Then, with the men peeing on the toilet and missing, I had to wipe all around it. From all the cooking Jada had done, she had the kitchen in a mess. She half cleaned it, so I went behind her to tidy it up. I made up our beds and straightened the closet. I also straightened the living room, where magazines were all over the place. Somebody left a can of soda on the table and an empty bag of Doritos was stuffed down in the couch. It was probably Prince because I saw him drinking from the soda can earlier.

Other than that, the place was back to normal. I was glad about that. I had to do this all over again tomorrow because my name was on the schedule for the next two days.

"Smelling good around here, ma," Roc said, referring to the smell of Pine-Sol as he stood in the bathroom's doorway. "I need to take a leak. Do you mind?"

"No," I said, quickly washing my hands and leaving the bathroom. I went to the kitchen to put the bucket and cleaning items underneath the sink and then threw away the gloves. I hurried back to the bathroom to catch Roc. As soon as he came out, there I was.

"What's up?" he said, rubbing his waves to flatten the front of them.

"Just wondering what you were up to. Thought we could go to the gym to work out, if you're not too busy."

"I was hangin' outside by the pool with everybody else and gettin' crunk off some music. If you want to work out, that sounds like a plan to me. Let me go change clothes."

I followed Roc into the bedroom. We went into the closet to get our workout gear, and then we sat on our beds to change. I stripped down to my lime-green boyshorts that didn't hide much. I didn't have on a bra and had no intentions to put one on. Roc changed into his Nike shorts and a T-shirt. He bent down to tie his tennis shoes, and that was when I stepped up to him. I stood in front of him half-naked and rubbed his waves. He inched his head up and glared at me.

"I thought you said you wanted to go work out," he said, removing my hands from his hair.

"I do want to, but I thought we could possibly start our work-out in here."

Roc lowered his eyes to my breasts that stared him right in the face. My nipples damn near touched the edge of his lips. When I felt his hand touch my leg, I figured I was in business. I leaned forward, causing him to lie back on the bed. Having his attention, I straddled him and sat directly on top of the steel he was packing. I could already feel it lying long between my coochie lips, and the feel of it had me hyped. His strong hands continued to roam my curves while he looked up at me.

"Riddle me this," he queried. "Why you sweatin' me? I already told you that I'm not sure about doin' this with you. And there is no doubt that my woman wouldn't approve of this."

"Sweetheart, I don't sweat men. I fuck them—well. The question is who's going to tell the woman you say you love? You? I know not me, so what are you so worried about? Plus, even though you're saying you don't want to do this, your actions say otherwise. You've been flip-flopping too much, Roc, and you really need to stop teasing me."

Roc was quiet—he was in thought, so I started to massage his rock-solid chest that was bulging with muscles. It was carved to near perfection and whoever his woman was, she was damn lucky to have all of him in bed with her every single night. I only had him now, so I intended to take full advantage of the moment.

As I massaged Roc's chest, his eyes fluttered and then closed. I leaned forward, placing the tips of my nipples on his chest while my ass was in midair. His hands were still roaming my backside, and then I felt his finger slide underneath my boyshorts. He found my wet spot and wasted no time sinking his finger inside of me. I had to tighten my lips to muffle my mouth as he went deeper. His touch had already started to make me rain. My inner thighs were wet; so wet that he made mention of it.

"Umph, exactly how I like it. Wet and warm," he said, inserting another finger for more pleasure.

"Rip them off. My boyshorts, that is."

Roc wrapped his fingers around the crotch section of my boyshorts and pulled tight. They ripped apart and he now had a clear path to my goodies. He still seemed a little hesitant, so I made the next move. I went for a kiss. A juicy one that hopefully took his mind off whatever or whoever it was he was thinking about. I sucked his tongue and licked his lips with as much passion as I could. That was when I felt him touch his shorts and slide them down. But as soon as he did, the bedroom door flew open. Our heads snapped to the side and we saw Jaylin walk into the room. He studied my ass, only for a few seconds, and then kept it moving.

"Didn't mean to interrupt," he said, going into the closet. He got something from it and then walked by us as if we weren't even there. He closed the door and my attention turned back to Roc. He sat up on his elbows to look me in the eyes.

"I'mma need to pull back on this, all right?"

I was shocked by his words, only because we were so close. This rejection bullshit was driving me nuts, and why did he keep messing with me like this? I hated a man who couldn't make up his mind, and to get me hyped like this was frustrating.

"Why do you want us to pull back? I'll go lock the door; that way no one else will interrupt us."

"No need to. I don't feel like this is somethin' I want to dig into right now. You bad, ma, fasho got it goin' on, but once I do a reality check, I gotta realize that I didn't come here for this."

"Neither did I, but since we're here, why not? I'm not going to sweat you, Roc, but why would you get me energized like this and then walk away? Are you okay with that?"

"Not really, but I'm not goin' to keep explainin' myself to you. Get up."

Okay, now it was a disrespect thing. Did he have to tell me to get up like that? I couldn't help but to think about what would've happened had Jaylin not come into the room. Damn him. I was mad, but sweating a man over his dick was not my style. I had already pushed this situation enough and this was it for me. Roc would have to make the next move.

I eased off him and sat in silence on the other bed to put on my clothes.

"Ay, you still want to work out, don't you?" Roc asked.

I shrugged. "Sure, why not?"

He told me to meet him in the workout area. Five minutes later, I did. We worked out for about an hour, and by that time, it was almost ten o'clock at night. Everybody had talked about turning in early, especially since we hadn't gotten much sleep last night. I was all for it because I was tired as hell.

"I'm gon' finish readin' the last few pages of this book, then I'm callin' it a night," Jada said.

"Hopefully you're readin' the dictionary," Prince said out loud.

"No, I'm not. But hopefully your uneducated, missin' tooth tail got one stuck up yo ass for me to borrow. If not, shut up and stop worryin' about what I'm doin'."

"Dang, girl, I was playin' with you. Why you always gettin' so hot and snippy with people?"

"Because you don't know me that well to be playin' with me. I'm a grown-ass woman, and I will not settle for bein' dissed by little boys who still pee in the bed." Jada cut her eyes at Prince and turned to Jaylin. "Boo, please keep my spot warm for me, and, Chase, don't forget to keep your mouth zipped tonight or we may have a repeat of yesterday."

I ignored Jada. She should've been reading every single dictionary in print, instead of a single book. Jaylin ignored her, too. I bet that bitch was a bully growing up, but even bullies got put in their places.

Within the next hour, I was finally ready to shut it down. Prince and Jada were the only two still awake. He was doing something on the computer and she was in the bathroom. I went into the bedroom and turned out the light. Jaylin was knocked completely out, but Roc was tossing and turning. Sylvia's eyes were closed, but she looked to be faking it.

I changed into my negligee and got in bed. Jada came in about ten minutes later. I kept my eyes opened, waiting for her to make some noise. I was so sure she would.

"Shit, it's cold in here," she said, putting on her pajamas and then laying down. I could hear her moving around in the bed. A cough followed and she fluffed her pillows. A few minutes later, she called Jaylin's name. "Sweetie, I have no idea what your last name is, but please, please get out of your bed now to see what this is."

Jaylin didn't say a word, but I heard him sigh.

"Oh. My, God!" She yelled. "What in the fuck is it?"

By now, everybody was up.

"Jada, this is a bunch of bullshit," Jaylin said, tossing his covers aside in anger. "What the fuck is your problem?"

"I don't know yet, but somethin' is in my damn bed!"

Since Roc was lying next to her, he shot out of the bed and turned on the light. Jada snatched the covers off of her, and to no surprise to me, there was a black rat snake slithering up the side of her fat, trembling leg.

She screamed at the top of her lungs and wiggled her legs around, trying to shake the snake off. Everybody else jumped back and no one seemed eager to get it. Even Prince had come into the room, but he stood far away by the doorway, telling others to "get that thing."

"Jaaaaylin!" Jada yelled. "Please get it, would you?"

Jaylin did not move. Sylvia was behind him standing on the bed, and Roc kept staring at the snake, carefully watching its every move. Jada was hysterical. She started crying, and when she rolled on the floor, so did the snake. She hopped up and busted out of the door so quickly that if you blinked, you missed her.

"Where did it go?" Sylvia asked, shaking like a leaf.

"It went underneath Roc's bed," Jaylin said. "Man, go get that thing and get it out of here."

Roc turned to Jaylin with a twisted face. "Muthafucka, are you crazy? I'm not fuckin' with that thing. Did you see how big it was?"

"I'm not fuckin' with it either," Prince said. "Somebody needs to call that white boy, Jeff, to see if he'll come get it out of here. Until then, my ass is not sleepin' in this bedroom."

They all were cowards. I was surprised, but what should I have expected from a bunch of pretty boys who knew nothing about the wilderness. A rat snake wasn't poisonous. It was just as afraid of them, as they were of it.

I had to be the brave one here, so I got on the floor and shooed the snake from underneath the bed with my pillow. When it slithered out, I grabbed it close to the head and picked it up. Jaylin and Roc looked at me as if I were crazy.

"Now we can all sleep tight," I said, carrying the snake through the house so I could put it in the backyard where I had found it earlier. Jada stood shaking in the kitchen. I couldn't resist stopping to say a few words to her. I used the snake as ammunition while holding its head close to her face.

"The next time you say anything else inappropriate to me, or put your hands on me, I'm going to shove this thing up your ass. As your friend Jaylin would say, you've been warned."

Jada was a bunch of mouth and she didn't have two words to say to me with the snake still in my hand. She rushed toward the front of the house, trying to get as far away from me as she could. I took the snake out back, and when I let it go, it slithered away. It was what I needed to make my point. From here on out, I was positive that Jada would think twice before going there with me again. I was the type of chick who didn't play, and this was a lesson learned for everyone inside the house.

Jaylin

It was another sleepless night for me. There was no way I could rest well, after that snake being in the house. I didn't get down with shit like that, and night after night, I kept thinking that something was crawling on me. Jada had called on the wrong person for help, and I was glad she handled that by falling on the floor. Eventually, I probably would've dealt with it, but when Chase picked that thing up without hesitating, it messed me up. She was brave, and I didn't see her as being that kind of woman.

The only reason it mattered was because the fellas and I were so sure that we could knock the women out of this house in a one-two-three punch. I wasn't so sure about that now; Chase had a courageous side to her that said she could handle anything. Three days later, we sat outside eating breakfast and contemplating our next move.

"I'm tellin' y'all she ain't goin' down like pooky and them," Roc said playfully in a whisper. "Did you see the way she manhandled that thing the other night?"

"I saw it," Prince said. "And I also saw yo scary punk ass. Nigga, I thought you had some balls."

"I got the amount that I need right here, so silence yourself," Roc said, grabbing himself down below. "If she hadn't rushed by me to go get it, I was on my way to pull that mutha from underneath my bed."

Prince didn't believe Roc and neither did I. "You were looking pretty scared to me, too," I said, adding my two cents. "I guess that was something the streets didn't teach you."

"Both of you niggas better lay off. Y'all were about to get ghost, and Jada was askin' for your help, Jaylin, not mine."

"Jada needed to be taught a lesson and she got a big one that night. But on another note, I doubt that she'll be starting shit with Chase again. The strategy was to keep them at each other, but for the last few days, I see things dying down a bit."

"It has been," Roc agreed. "But when all is said and done, Chase is gangsta. She ain't got it all upstairs, for real."

"Gangsta and gutter," Prince added. "That bitch got it, but she's psycho."

We all agreed and Roc continued on. "I've been playin' her off, hopin' that she'll get tired of my rejection and get the fuck out of here. You've been ignorin' her, and her and Prince have no connection whatsoever. I don't understand why she's still here. One hundred G's ain't really that much money to brag about. She told me that bein' the last person standin' wasn't important. If it ain't, what's keepin' her here?"

"You," I said. "Maybe me, too, but I say make a move on it. Work your magic and pretend as if you're falling for her. Then, tell her it's imperative that she leaves."

"Why me?" Roc asked. "You say make a move, but what kind of move? How far do you fools expect me to go?"

"All the way," Prince said. "She may be a snake-handler, but all women got some kind of weakness. Break her ass down 'cause we need to start now in gettin' them out of the way. Then, I can work on y'all."

"That ain't gon' happen, Prince, so you can erase that from your head," I said and then looked at Roc. "You need to go all the way with her. What's the hold up anyway? As good as that ass was looking the other day you should've knocked that pussy out of the box."

"I'm tryin' to hold back, but why ain't you hittin' it? You know what's up with me and you may have better luck than I do. She ridin' yo nuts, too."

"Not like she's riding yours, and let's not forget that you had that pussy in your hands. I didn't. But whatever it takes, I'm with it. Whoever gets there first, so be it. But whichever one of us do go there, we need to work fast on getting her out of here. She's the biggest challenge for us."

"Fasho," Roc said. "What about Sylvia?"

"Fuck Sylvia. I see her as the weakest link. She's been feeling guilty about going through my things, and I can see her weakening by the day. She won't last. When I get done with her, she'll be walking real soon."

"Jada?" Prince said.

"We need Jada to cook for us." Roc laughed. "She'll be the last to go."

We all bumped fists and headed to the court to play a game of basketball.

Later that day, I sat in the living room watching TV by myself. The others were all outside chilling somewhere, but I couldn't exactly pinpoint what they were doing. Nobody wanted to get into politics with me, so I was tuned into *The Ed Show*, trying to see what was up. Those sly-ass Republicans were trying to make all kinds of excuses for the new voter suppression laws and intimidation that had gone on before and after the election. They weren't willing to compromise with the President on shit, and I was listening to an elderly woman speak about how she had been voting for years, but had found it difficult to do. As I was tuned in, Sylvia came over to the couch with her swimming suit on and a towel was wrapped around her. She was shivering.

"Why is it always so cold in here?" she asked.

All I did was shrug. First, because I was interested in what the lady on TV was saying. Also, I was still upset with Sylvia for going through my things. Then there was a little thing called strategy. I had to play her like this, if I wanted her to leave.

"Are you not speaking to me anymore?" she questioned.

"Can't you see I'm busy watching TV?"

"Yes, but watching TV or not, you still haven't said much to me. I don't know what else you want me to say. I've already apologized to you, Jaylin, so stop being so ridiculous about this."

"Apology not accepted because you had no business going through my shit. Why would you do that anyway? That was some bold mess, baby. Even the lady in my life don't get down like that."

She sighed and raked her fingers through her braids. "I...I was just looking for something. Wanted to see if—"

I cocked my head back in disbelief that she was making excuses. "Looking for what? In my pockets? What could you be looking for in a man's pockets? What you're saying makes no sense to me, and what you really need to do is move away from me. Keep your distance for the remainder of your stay. I'll be good with that. Trust and believe."

Sylvia sucked her teeth and glared at me. "I should've known that coming here was a big mistake. Thought it would do me some good, but being here has been even more messed up. It was nice knowing you, Jaylin. I'm out of here and good riddance."

Sylvia ranted as she walked away and headed for the bedroom. She moved so fast that I'm sure she didn't see the wicked grin on my face. Yes, I felt a little bad about the shit, but this was serious business; no time for real pleasure. Plus, I was really ticked about what she had done. I didn't trust her not one bit, so I was glad she was leaving. So glad that I was eager to go outside to tell Roc and Prince the good news. I had done my part. Now, it was time for them to step up and do theirs.

Before going outside, I went to the bedroom to make sure Sylvia was packing. She was. She looked mad as hell, but I had seen many upset women in my lifetime. That didn't faze me one bit, unless it was Nokea. Sometimes, Scorpio.

"You are such a loser," she said, throwing a pair of shoes in her suitcase. "I'm so glad that I didn't give myself to you the other night and what a big mistake that would've been."

"The feeling is mutual," I said, pretending to look for something in the closet. "Just stop the griping and hurry up, get your shit and go."

"You don't have to tell me twice. When all is said and done, you're the one who is going to get screwed. I tried to spare you, but you're so darn blind that you don't even realize you're being set up. And let's not forget about how arrogant you are. You think you know it all, but the truth is, you don't know jack."

She had my attention. I swung around and looked at her. "What in the hell are you talking about? Set up how?"

"I'm sure you would like to know!" She picked up one piece of her luggage and carried it into the bedroom. I followed, and when she tried to walk by me, I grabbed her arm.

"If you know something, you need to tell me. Now," I demanded.

"I'm not telling you anything. Not after the way you treated me. Are you serious?"

Sylvia tried to get away from my grip, but I squeezed tighter on her arm. "I need to know right now what's up. Maybe I did go overboard with what I said to you, but that was because—"

"Because you're an asshole. Now, let my arm go, Jaylin, before I call someone in here and have you arrested for harassing me."

Her words upset me. I frowned and loosened my grip on her arm. "Ain't nobody harassing you. All I want to know is what in the hell it is that you're talking about?"

She folded her arms in front of her. "If you want to know, then apologize to me."

"For what? I said maybe I went overboard, didn't I?"

Her hand moved to her hip and her neck rolled. "That is not an apology and you know it. Is it that hard for you to say you're sorry to someone, especially when you know you're wrong?"

"You haven't convinced me that I'm wrong yet, have you?"

Sylvia swallowed and turned away from me. I could tell she knew something, but she was reluctant to say what it was. My blood was boiling by the minute. I was seconds away from doing something I really didn't want to do.

"Tell me, *baby*," I said, softening my tone and pleading with her in a calm manner. "Please tell me. If something ain't right here, I need to know. Don't you want me to know?"

She turned around to face me. "I didn't want you and Roc to get into a fight because I knew it would be bad. I really wanted you to stay in this house, and I was afraid that if the two of you got into a fistfight, Jeff would kick you out. I like you, Jaylin, and—"

"Then, stop beating around the fuck—the bush and eliminate all this mumbo jumbo. Of course you like me, but I'm not interested in hearing all of that right now. Get to the point."

Sylvia's tone went up a notch and she pointed her finger at me. "You are being played. I wasn't the one who went through your things, Prince was. I saw him searching through your stuff, but he didn't see me. I saw him turning the combination to your safe, but he couldn't get it to open. And as for your letter, I saw him read it and throw it in the trashcan. It wasn't me, Jaylin, it was him. So you need to watch your back around here, instead of laughing and lollygagging with everybody. I thought you were much smarter than that, but then again, I've been known to be wrong about some things, especially when it comes to men."

By now, locomotive steam was shooting from my ears and I was stroking my goatee hard. I couldn't believe these mother-fuckers were trying to play me. I was sure Roc was in on it, too. I didn't have time to thank Sylvia for the information. I rushed out of the bedroom, looking for both of those fools to show them what happened to people who fucked with me.

Jada

I had gotten over the ordeal with the snake incident the other day. Chase and I were barely speaking to each other, and the last thing I wanted to do was bump heads with a bitch who didn't mind being in the wilderness. I mean, there was something eerie about a woman who could manhandle a snake. I kept my distance, but the door was still open for her to get her butt whooped again.

I was outside on the patio doing the bump with Roc, while the music was blasting. We were having so much fun. He couldn't believe how low I could go to the ground, but I had been there several times and was working my way back up. My fingers were in the air, and I was popping them to the beat of "Da' Butt."

"Aww, shit," Roc said, playfully smacking my ass, as I bent over and danced. We were clowning. Everybody else was drinking and laughing their butts off. Not to mention that a few of us were high. Me, Roc and Prince had fired up a joint in the bathroom about an hour ago and were blazing.

The song switched to Soulja Boy's "Crank That" and everybody was on their feet, especially Prince who knew the lyrics word for word. He was saying them out loudly, bobbing his head and dancing close to Chase. She was laughing her behind off and seemed to get a kick out of Prince's suave moves. I kept clowning and dancing so wildly that I twisted my damn ankle and stumbled to break my fall. It was a good thing that Roc caught me, or else I would've been on my ass. I limped over to a chair, but before I could take a seat, a hurricane blew through the backyard. At least that was what I thought it was, but instead, it was Jaylin storming out of the sliding door and looking like a madman. He blew by me and his eyes moved across the patio until they came in contact with his target. He crept up on Prince like a thief in the night. Grabbed him by his shirt and slung him around. Within seconds, Prince was on the ground.

"Muthafucka, you've been going through my shit, haven't you? You want to steal something from me, huh? Is that what you trying to do?"

Jaylin shook Prince by the collar and drug him to the edge of the pool. He dunked Prince's face into the water as if he was waterboarding his ass like a terrorist. Prince was so high that he didn't know if he was coming or going. I suspected his body had to be hurting from hitting the ground so hard, and he was choking on the water because Jaylin kept dunking him.

"Stop it, Jaylin!" Sylvia yelled in a panic as she rushed outside. "You're going to kill him!"

That was when Roc ran over to pull Jaylin away from Prince. Now, what in the hell did he do that for? I don't know what had gotten into Jaylin, but I seriously thought the devil was upon us. He pushed Roc away from him and punched Prince in his midsection. Prince doubled over and rolled flat on his back.

"What the fuck is wrong with you, nigga?" Roc yelled, intervening again. But this time, Jaylin caught Roc in the face with a straight right hook—one that you would've thought only Muhammad Ali could deliver. I swear I heard Roc's jaw crack. The blow staggered him several inches backward, but from there, it was on. Roc lost it and went crazy. He charged at Jaylin, knocking him to the ground. They were pounding the shit out of each other. Grunting and talking shit.

"You want some of me, nigga, is that what you want?" Roc said as he had Jaylin in a headlock.

Jaylin used his elbow to jab Roc in the gut. "Yeah, I want some, but give me more!"

This was getting scary, but all we could do was back up and move out of the way. Nobody dared to get in the middle of that squabble; if they did, they would've gotten knocked the hell out.

Jaylin picked Roc up by his legs, carrying him a few feet and dropping him back first on one of the tables. It came crashing down and the umbrella fell on top of them. Roc's fists were like solid bricks as they went into Jaylin's body, and after another punch to Jaylin's face, that was when Roc drew blood. We couldn't call the police or nothing, and there seemed to be no end to the madness. Chase's hand covered her mouth, Sylvia had tears cascading down her face, and I was shaking all over because I thought somebody was going to die in front of me.

"Cut the bullshit, please!" I yelled, but neither of them listened. By now, all of the patio furniture was scattered. Some was broken into pieces and some was floating in the pool. Jaylin had his hands around Roc's throat, squeezing so tight that as black as he was, his neck was turning red. Then all of a sudden, the producer, Jeff, and several big bodyguards came rushing outside. They did their best to separate Roc and Jaylin, but it was no easy task. It took all the manpower in sight to get some kind of order.

"Ladies, please go into the house," Jeff ordered. "I don't want anybody else to get hurt."

Without hesitating, me, Sylvia and Chase went inside. I was near speechless, only because I didn't want nothing like this to go down.

"I feel so bad," Sylvia said, easing back on the couch. "I shouldn't have said anything to Jaylin. I should've left like I had planned to."

"What did you say to him?" Chase said with an attitude.

"I told him the truth about who actually went through his things. It wasn't me; it was Prince. I saw him trying to steal from Jaylin, but I didn't tell him because I didn't want anything like this to happen. That's why I took the blame for it."

"I knew that slick, sticky-fingers fool was up to no good!" I said, referring to Prince. "I've been hidin' my stuff. If it were me, I probably would've clowned on his ass, too. All these niggas out here do is take, take, take. I don't understand what Roc had to do with it, though."

"I'm not sure," Sylvia said. "But I didn't tell Jaylin anything about Roc. He assumed that Roc and Prince were conspiring against him."

"They probably were," Chase said. "But here's what you ladies need to know, so wake up and pay attention. I overheard them talking. They've been plotting and scheming against us since we walked into this house. The objective was to get us out of here, so the three of them could be here together. They talked about who they believe the weakest link is, and unfortunately, Sylvia, that title belongs to you. Jada, you're good for cooking, so they want to keep you around. They believe that if we keep arguing and fighting with each other, that's how one of them will win. I say we come up with a plan that will send them packing before we do."

My jaw dropped as Chase spoke. I couldn't believe they would do something so sneaky. Then again, it made sense. Men always stuck together, but they weren't representing that today.

"I guess that explains why Jaylin treated me like crap. He was pretty much delighted when I told him I was leaving earlier."

Sylvia folded her arms and moved back on the couch. "I'm all for what you ladies want to do. Please count me in because I'm not going anywhere."

"Neither am I," I said, adding my two cents. "And I wish those bastards would've killed each other out there. Maybe they'll get kicked out of here. If so, then all I'll have to deal with are the two of you."

"One person at a time," Chase said. "Keep quiet. They're coming inside."

Jaylin walked in first with fresh bloodstains on his deep purple polo shirt. I didn't know who the blood belonged to, probably both of them. His cargo shorts were ripped and his knuckles were bruised. His face didn't look too bad, other than his nose that was still dripping some blood. Two bodyguards came in after him, and then Prince came in next. Jeff and another dude were holding him up. Prince looked dazed as ever.

"Wha...where in the fuck am I?" Prince said, barely able to stand. I didn't know if the fool was playing games or not, especially since it was now revealed that they had been doing so all along.

Jeff helped Prince to the couch and he fell back on it. He closed his eyes and dropped his limp arm on his forehead. Roc came in next. His face looked a little puffy on the left, but it was hard to see any bruising because he was so damn black. His face was twisted with anger and he was still taking deep breaths.

Jeff addressed all of us at once. "This is an example of taking things too far. Let me know if we need to end this right now, or if all of you can somehow figure out a way to get along. If you can't, go ahead and leave now. The door is open for anyone who wants to leave and nobody will be held here against their will. If you decide to stay, there can't be a repeat of what happened here today. I'm not going to be responsible for anybody getting killed in here, and anyone who crosses the line again will be arrested. Do you hear me on that, Jaylin? You will be arrested."

"Do what you must do." Jaylin spoke in a calm manner, massaging his hands together. He seemed unfazed by all that had happened. Roc appeared way angrier than him. "I'm not going anywhere, and nobody in here is going to make me leave. If you don't wish to witness a repeat of what happened here, please remind these assholes that trying to take from another man will bring about trouble."

"Take what?" Roc said, holding out his hands and moving forward. One of the bodyguards stood in front of him. "Nigga, you ain't got a damn thing that I want, or for that matter, can't get. That's on a for real tip right there, so stop talkin' that madness about the next man tryin' to take somethin' from you, other than a stupid-ass love letter from yo bitch that got you all choked up around here."

Jaylin rubbed his goatee and looked at Roc with a smirk. "Go sit the fuck down or go learn how to throw some punches that sting. You hit like a bitch, and if I didn't know any better, I'd think you had a pussy."

"Gentlemen, please," Jeff said, looking at Roc. "Is this over for you? Are you done here?"

"Fuck naw, I'm not done. Come see me in three months. This is where I will be."

Roc walked off and Jaylin sat back on the couch with his arms resting on top of it. It looked like we were in for a long three months; at this point, nobody was budging. I hated to see black men go at each other like this and Lord knows I witnessed this time and time again with Kiley and his friends. There were plenty of times where I was caught in the middle and there were times that I regretted not having Kiley's back like I should've. For the moment, I changed my mind about plotting with Sylvia and Chase; them hoes couldn't be trusted either. I had Jaylin's back, even though the men had been plotting. I would've had Roc's back, too, if he had not gone into the other room.

"What'cha need, baby?" I said sitting next to Jaylin on the couch, trying to get a smile out of him. "You want me to get you a clean shirt or fix you somethin' good to eat?"

Jaylin glanced at the bloodstain on his shirt and then he pulled it over his head. He laid the shirt on his lap and eyeballed Jeff and his bodyguards as they went outside to talk. Sylvia and Chase walked away as well.

"Nah, sweetheart, I don't need anything from you. I had some frustrations that I needed to let out, so I did. Unfortunately, it's hard for me to do backstabbing people, and I regret that you ladies had to witness me getting down like that." Jaylin looked over at Prince on the couch. His eyes were still closed.

"No need to apologize, but I don't like to see brothas go at it like that. Y'all were gettin' it in. I thought y'all would kill each other."

"It could've come to that, but thankfully, it didn't. But I don't want to talk about what happened. It's a done deal and both of those fools now know where I stand. My question to you is, what can I do for you? You've been real sweet to me, with the exception of farting on me and cooking me fatty foods."

I couldn't help but laugh and blush at the same time. "That fart slipped, Jaylin. I didn't try to do that, and you know darn well that you like my food. As for what you can do for me...I can think of a whole lot of things, but I don't know if you'll be able to handle my requests."

Jaylin rubbed his chin and winked at me. "Anything. I'm good at granting requests, especially if they're good ones."

I cocked my head back. "I don't know where you're goin' with this, but you can keep that big dick in your pants. I'm not ready for that."

He grinned and shrugged his shoulders. "My dick don't come that easy, but you can have something else."

"Well, okay, Mr. Richy Rich. I want you to leave this house so I can win the hundred thousand dollars. You're goin' to be the hardest person to beat, and it's obvious that you don't need the money. Plus, I want you to eat the entire plate of whatever I cook and rub my achy feet with those strong hands, too."

"If you win, you win on your own, so that request is denied. And it depends on what's on that plate, if I'll eat it all. Your feet? Let me get a close-up look at them."

I removed one foot from my sandal and placed it on Jaylin's lap. He frowned. "Listen," I said. "You asked me what I wanted and I told you. Can a sista get somethin' out of you?"

Jaylin spread my toes and pointed in between them. "Your toes are polished, but they still crusty as hell. Your heels, I won't even comment on those, so I prefer to eat the food."

I wiggled my toes on his lap and moved them close to his lips. He backed his head up and smacked my feet away from him. "Don't play with me like that, all right?" His look was stern. I could tell he didn't like that, but I pouted.

"Geesh, I guess I'd better come up with requests that suit you, not me, huh?"

"No, but here's the deal. If you somehow manage to win this challenge, I'll give you an extra hundred thousand dollars. And if you cook me a healthy meal, I'll massage your feet and work some of that crust off them. Let me know if we have a deal."

I threw my hand back at him. "You know damn well that you won't give me that kind of money if I win, will you?"

Jaylin held out his hand to shake mine. "My word, my bond. Now, go cook my food before I change my mind about those feet."

We shook on his deal. I got off the couch and rushed to the kitchen to prepare Jaylin a healthy meal. This time, I grilled some chicken with mixed vegetables and made a low-fat chocolate pudding that would make his mouth water. After Jeff and the bodyguards left, Jaylin threw down in the kitchen. He gave me a pat on the back, and on my ass and then he worked my feet over like a professional. Worked them so good that I damn near creamed in my panties. I fanned myself with my hand and squirmed around on the couch.

"Oooo, ahh, uh-oh, hold the hell up," I said, trying to sit up straight as I felt a tickle and a trickle at the same time.

Jaylin continued to rub lotion in all the right places. "Wha... what's wrong with you?" he asked.

Goose bumps appeared on my arms, so I pulled my feet back and clamped my legs together. "Tha...that's enough, boo. I'm good. Thanks, though, okay?"

Jaylin had a wicked grin on his face. He must have known what his hands were capable of doing. I had to hurry to the bathroom and get my pussy in check. *She* knew better than clowning like that, didn't *she*? If *she* didn't, maybe I needed to reiterate my plan. It was to approach Roc and Jaylin differently than Chase and Sylvia had. I was sure that the way to warming Jaylin's heart was through money, not by throwing pussy at him. No degree or advanced education taught me that, and I had gotten my knowledge from the streets. The streets also taught me how to play to win. With a possible extra hundred grand in my pocket, winning had become the priority and it was time to stop playing with these hoes, Sylvia and Chase. Not matter what they believed, we were not in this together.

Sylvia

What a day this truly was. Roc and Jaylin hadn't said anything to each other, and Prince was so messed up that he was now in the bed knocked out. Jada said he had smoked some weed and drunk a lot of alcohol. I was sure that it played a big part as to why he was still out of it. I mean, Jaylin had messed him up, no doubt, but Prince kind of deserved it. He thought he was being slick, and I should've said something when I initially saw him going through Jaylin's things. I was sure Prince had searched through other people's belongings, but I thought if I warned him, that it would be enough for him to back off.

No matter what, I was still upset that the men thought I was the weakest link. That hurt my feelings a bit, but I guess it was because of the way I had come across. If only they got a chance to know the real Sylvia McMillan. The one I used to be, years ago, when I didn't give a care about anything. I spent the last year or so trying to make myself over. Trying not to hold grudges and trying to forgive those who had wronged me as well. I didn't want to be selfish anymore, and I started praying every day for God to give me the strength to better myself. I had made much progress, but to men, that progress made me look weak. No wonder when I had gone to see Jonathan he really didn't have much to say. My new attitude was a turnoff to him. He told me he was getting married again and said that he was happier than he'd been in his entire life. Hearing him say that to me really hurt. But all I could do was congratulate him and wish him well.

Dealing with all of that was what brought me here and into Jaylin's presence. I had pushed my thoughts of Jonathan to the back of my mind, until I realized that the two of them were friends. Out of respect for myself, I said I didn't want to go there. I told myself that Jaylin was off limits. But I started to think not. Jonathan was a part of my past that I wanted to forget. He could not care less who I was with, and I doubted that having sex with Jaylin would hurt Jonathan. I couldn't remember him and Jaylin being that close. Their connection seemed more about business than anything. At least, that was what I kept telling myself, but then today happened. I found out that I was being used. Jaylin had toyed with my emotions in order to get me out of this house. He was going to have sex with me and then literally kick me in my ass and tell me to get to packing. In no way did I expect him to have feelings for me, but that was cold. There seemed like a lot of passion between us in that bathroom, and I figured he was into the moment just as much as I was.

Then I had to consider playing the same game with him, as he'd played with me. Chase and Jada wanted revenge. They were plotting to get back at the men, and the only way we could weaken them was through the most powerful thing we had to offer. Sex. Sex, Chase said, would break them down. It would confuse them and have them eating out of the palms of our hands. Good sex would throw them off track and make them forget about winning this challenge altogether, Jada said. But when I asked who would be willing to put themselves out there like that, Jada said not her. The seducing would be left up to Chase and me. Jada, on the other hand, would make Prince think that she was so interested in him that he would want to leave this house with her and go get married.

Well, I wasn't foolish enough to underestimate any of these men, and I started to renege on our plans. Truthfully, I didn't trust Chase or Jada. I didn't tell them that I didn't, nor did I tell them that I'd be playing by my own darn rules. If I was going to win this challenge, it would be because of my own strategic planning. No one would get credit, and to hell with them all for considering me to be the weakest link.

At two o'clock in the morning, I couldn't sleep. I tossed and turned in bed, noticing that Jaylin wasn't beside me in his bed. While in my cream, silk shorts and pajama top, I left the bedroom to go find him. I spotted him standing in the kitchen drinking from a small carton of chocolate milk. He was in his Calvin Klein briefs and nothing else. I stood for a moment to check him out from a side view. His sexy abs moved in and out each time he swallowed. His package was sitting real pretty, and I swear that man had one hell of a bulge. I wanted to jump right on it, but all I did was clear my throat to get his attention. He removed the carton from his lips and turned his head.

"I didn't see you standing there," he said and then tossed the empty carton in the trashcan.

"It wasn't for long. But long enough for me to realize why I'm so attracted to you."

Jaylin nudged his head toward the backyard. "Let's go outside and talk."

I followed him to the backyard, where he sat near the edge of the pool and put his feet in the water. So did I. He told me that he was having a difficult time sleeping.

"I couldn't get a lick of sleep either," I said, looking straight ahead at the waterfall in front of us. "That waterfall is a beautiful sight, isn't it?"

Jaylin shrugged and then yawned. Sitting close to him, I noticed a small cut near his chin and his hands looked battered. Several bruises were on his chest. "The waterfall is nice," he said. "But it would be even better if a hot tub or bar was behind there."

"I agree and it makes no sense for someone to create all of this and not include, at least, a hot tub."

It was apparent that we were making small talk; seconds later, silence soaked the backyard. I figured Jaylin didn't want to talk much, but I had a lot on my mind that I wanted to say to him. I regretted that because of me, him, Roc and Prince went at it. I also wanted to find out why he considered me to be the weakest link.

"I know you don't feel like talking much right now, but what's on your mind?" I asked. "Why can't you sleep?"

"I'm always a night owl, and, sometimes, I don't sleep at all. I thought I'd be able to get some rest in this place, but it's kind of hard sleeping next to a fool who tried to take from me."

"I get that. However, what I don't understand is why you went after Roc? I didn't tell you that he had done anything wrong, but you went after him like he was the one responsible for messing with your things."

"That's not true. I went after Prince. Roc intervened when he shouldn't have. If he had stayed back, I probably wouldn't have said anything to him. Then again, I have a feeling that him and Prince been trying to get at me since day one."

"We've all been trying to get at each other since day one. That was the plan, wasn't it? The plan has always been for you all to knock us out of the competition first, right? And since I was considered the weakest link, I'd be the first to go."

Jaylin looked at me, wondering where I got my information. He didn't ask, but I let him off the hook.

"Don't worry about how I know what I do, but I'll say this. I'm far from being weak and shame on you for thinking so. If there was anybody's back in this house I had, it was yours. Just like you, Prince and Roc, Jada and Chase are up to no good, too. What they're conspiring to do, I want no part of it. If I'm going to win this challenge, I want to win it fair and square. I'm not going down without a good fight, and I can assure you that the men in this house will not be the last three standing."

Jaylin reached out to shake my hand. I welcomed it and shook his. "I appreciate you for telling me all of that. I will start watching my back a little better and keep my eyes on things. Normally, I do, but for some reason I'm slipping. As for you being the last person here, good luck with that."

"Thanks," I said, laughing. "But why? Why are you slipping and what's your story, Jaylin? You appear to have a lot going on, and I don't know if that's a good or bad thing."

Jaylin stood and stretched. He yawned and then sat on one of the lounge chairs that weren't broken from the fight he had with Roc. "It's actually a good thing," he said. "I love my life...really, I do. But my circle of friends is small and it can get lonely at the top sometimes. My ex-wife and I have had our share of problems, but at the end of the day, she will always be my future. I haven't forgiven her for some of the things she's done, but I'll get over it one day."

"Well, in order for you to get the peace you need, you'll have to forgive her. There is no other way, but you'll have to do so on your time, not mine."

Jaylin nodded his head and yawned again.

"If you're tired, why don't you go get some sleep?" I suggested.

"I will, but I'm enjoying our conversation right now, if that's okay with you? Come here."

I went over to where he was, and instead of sitting next to him, I sat on the edge of the lounge chair in between his spread legs. "What is it that you want from me, Sylvia?" he said. "Whatever it is, it's all in your eyes and caught up in your throat. Speak now or hold your peace."

I smiled and regretted that he could read me so well. "Nothing much, but I've been thinking about this entire thing with you and Jonathan. Been thinking about our heated session in the bathroom and I've come to a conclusion."

"Yeah. And what might that be?"

"I don't care what Jonathan or anybody thinks about what I do on my watch. Jonathan will soon be a married man again, and I must move on and live my life as well. Do you understand what I'm saying?"

"I believe so. You're saying to hell with Jonathan and you're giving me permission to tap that ass. I also assume you won't have any regrets."

"That's exactly what I'm saying. Thanks for reading my mind. I don't think I could've said it any better."

Jaylin got quiet for a minute, and then he spoke up. "I'm down with it, Sylvia, but hear me out on this. Whatever happens between us inside this house will not go any further. I'm not leaving this house and adding another woman to my circle of friends. I will not make myself available for communications, and once you or I walk out that door, I do not want to see you again. No offense, but it has to be this way. Understood?"

"Understood very well. And just so you know, I wouldn't have it any other way."

"Good. Now, let's go inside to get some sleep. My body is aching too much right now to get into the groove that I would like to with you. Give me another day or two and I'll be ready to paint them walls all over."

"I hope you will be. I'll be waiting breathlessly, in hopes that you and Roc can get along and we can pick up where we left off."

Jaylin took my hand and we went into the house together. I slept in his bed and finally got the rest I needed.

Prince

Been a while since I got my ass kicked like that, but they don't call me a Street Soldier for nothing. I could take the pain and bounce back as if a beat-down never happened. Just like I did when a so-called friend of mine set me up to be robbed. What Jaylin had done to me didn't come close to what that fool had done, and when it came to certain niggas on the streets, take my word for it, they were ruthless.

I was at a pizza joint that day, chilling with some friends. After the chicks from school left, my partner, Cedric, said he was going to take a leak and would be right back. I waited for him, and then we walked outside to our cars. We talked for a while, and it wasn't long before he got into his car and jetted. I pulled on the door handle to open my car door, and that was when a brotha who was dark as midnight approached me. A cigarette dangled from his mouth and he asked if I had a light.

"Naw, bruh, I ain't got nothin'."

I gazed into his sneaky eyes, knowing immediately that something wasn't right. If anything, I knew what a thief in the night looked like; I had been classified as that kind of manic before, too. I wasn't quick enough, though, and by the time I made my move for the door, a shiny blade was being pressed against my neck. He twisted my arm behind my back, causing severe pain to shoot up my arm. I was asked to empty my pockets, and he threatened to slice my throat if I didn't cooperate.

Since the blade was pinching my neck, I abided by his rules, but that wasn't enough. He took the money from my pockets and he also took the paper he'd found inside of my car. With several G's stashed in his pockets, he caught me off guard when he tore into my stomach with powerful blows that sent me staggering to my knees. I covered my face and tried to shield his numerous blows, but his punches became too much for me. All I could feel were street soldier marks being formed on my body, and after a while, my whole body felt numb from him kicking it. My face was scratched to the flesh from it hitting the ground so hard. I could barely see out of my nearly shut eye, and I seriously thought I was about to die. I laid there helpless as he stomped the shit out of me and left me for dead. If it weren't for a man who came outside of the pizza joint and threatened to call the police, I probably would have been dead. Thanks to him, I was able to crawl into my car and drive home. That was when I found out that the whole damn thing was a set up. My boy Cedric had set me up, and he had the nerve to go back to the pizza joint to retrieve the money that had been placed in the dumpster for him to get it. He didn't think I was well enough to follow him, but broken ribs or not, I followed him. As soon as he had the bag of money gripped in his hand, I blew his fucking brains out. I didn't even stay around to see his body drop, but with blood gushing from my mouth, and a deep cut along the side of my face, I had to get to Mama's house soon so she could clean me up.

Just like that fool had done, Pretty Boy, Jaylin, caught me tripping. I was high and intoxicated—slipping more like it. I should've known better, and, truthfully, I didn't think that punk had all of that in him. I was surprised that he was able to go toe-to-toe with Roc, and neither one of those fools came out as real winners. The real winner was me because I was alive.

It was strange, though, that everybody thought I was this no-good fool, looking for trouble. I wasn't. I used to gank people for their shit, but I stopped doing that kind of mess. I almost lost my life, again, when these fools shot up my car. My son and his mother were in the car with me that day and it ended up being a tragedy. Along with that, my partner, Romeo, was doing years in the pen for burglary and attempted murder. And when they sentenced him that day, it was my wakeup call.

With Jaylin, I did want to see how much cash he had on him, but I was also trying to see what I could find out about him. A rich nigga like that sparked my curiosity. I saw his safe and was curious to see what was in there. If anything, I wanted to see how I could be down. I think he was swoll about the letter more than anything. I guess it meant something to him, and I shouldn't have thrown it away. His daughter had written him a little something special, too, and I was sure he was disappointed to find the letter in the trash. The only reason I had thrown it away was because I had spilt some juice on it. I didn't want him to know I had read it, but what the hell? It was a done deal now. All I could do was holla at the man about my fuck ups, and I had no problem owning up to my shit. If Jaylin refused to listen, too bad. Time to move on.

We had all slept late, and I was in the bathroom getting it in. I didn't know where everybody else was, but Roc was in the kitchen cooking since he was on the schedule to do it. I could also smell something burning, so I suspected everybody would be gaming for Jada to return to the kitchen and cook us something good to eat.

After handling my business in the bathroom, I opened the door to leave. Jada was at the door with a wide smile on her face. "Did anybody ever tell you that you look like Trey Songz?" she said to me.

What she said came as no surprise to me. "Yep. However, I'd like to think that I got more swag than he do."

"Oh, trust me when I say you do, boo. You really and truly do.

Keep up the good work 'cause havin' those kinds of looks may be beneficiary to you."

Now, I wasn't proclaiming to be no teacher, professor or anything like that, nor did I have a high school diploma. But I hated a dumb bitch. Didn't Jada know that the word she was grasping for was beneficial? I didn't dare correct her; her mouth was slick and I'd have to beat that ass for saying the wrong thing. My goal was to get along with everybody, so I winked at Jada and walked away to go find out where Jaylin was.

Jada went into the bathroom and closed the door. I heard her say, "Damn, it stinks in here! Smells like somebody done died, and what done crawled out of yo ass, boy!"

I cracked up, blaming her for making those enchiladas and grilled chicken last night. Didn't she know that what goes in must come out? Mexican food wasn't nothing to play with, especially when it was cooked up and served by a black woman. As usual, she had thrown down.

I saw Roc standing shirtless in the kitchen putting bread in the toaster. By the look on his face, he still looked heated about yesterday, so I was reluctant to ask if he'd seen Jaylin. I went for it.

"Have you seen Pretty Boy around here? I wanted to find him so I could make peace with him about messin' with his stuff. Wanted to get at you, too, for puttin' yourself in the middle. I appreciate it, but understand that I didn't want nothin' to go down like it did. My bad, all right?"

"No, it ain't all right. And if both of you niggas were in the streets, on my turf, you'd be dead right now. Good luck with your search."

I said nothing else to bitter brother; he obviously needed more time to cool off. I hated a fool to talk mess about what they would do, if this or that, and my whole thing was if you were going to do something, then do it. Threatening people made me get tight, and Roc didn't want me to lose complete respect for him. I already didn't have much, so he had better watch what he said to me from here on out.

I figured I would find Jaylin exercising in the workout area and that was where he was. I mean, this dude worked out faithfully. He said he played a lot of golf and basketball too, but I didn't know how to play golf to save my soul. I did know how to pump iron, though, so I sat on a weight bench far away from him, in case he wanted to get at me again. He was doing some sit-ups, ignoring me.

"Do you know where the remote is so I can turn up the TV?" I asked him.

He didn't respond. Kept doing his sit-ups and grunted louder. I sat back to lift some weights, but when I looked up, I saw him standing over me.

"You got some issues," he said. "Fix them, before they get you severely hurt."

I placed the weights back on the bar and sat up. Lowered my head some and placed my elbows on my knees. "Truthfully," I said. "We all got issues, but I was wrong for goin' through yo things. I know you don't believe me, but all I was doin' was tryin' to check you out. You look like you're in a position where I'm tryin' to be. Wanted to see what was up with you 'cause I wasn't gon' ask."

"If you don't ask, then how else will you know? That's the problem with y'all young people today. Think y'all know it all and always trying to get away with slick shit. Too afraid to talk to somebody about what you're dealing with, especially people who are in a position to help you. It doesn't matter if I believe you or not, but I work hard for my shit, Prince. Real hard, and I ain't never stole nothing from nobody or took shit from the next man to get to where I am today. Yeah, I inherited some money, but that money only went so far. I've had to work my ass off, and I'll be damned if I let any fucking body take from me. When you take from me, you take from my family, especially my kids. I take that shit personal, so that's why you got the ass-kicking that you got yesterday. Next time, think before you act. Because if you don't, you'll be dead before you know it."

I shrugged. "What you're sayin' to me, I've heard before. It's nothin' new."

"Then let that shit sink in," Jaylin said, raising his voice. "Of course you've heard it before, but stop thinking that life is a fucking game and you can play it how you wish. You can't, and your parents should've taught you that taking from the next man has severe consequences. I guess all that talk about you being a businessman was a lie. I thought you had your head on straight, but I see that I was wrong."

"Don't bring my parents into this. Neither of them exists and they haven't for a long time. My father ain't shit and I don't have nothin' but hate in me for that nigga."

Jaylin held out his hands. "So, what you want me to do? Feel sorry for you? Negro, please. My mother died when I was nine and my father jetted the day of her funeral. I lived in an orphanage, and when I did get out, I was physically and mentally abused by my aunt and her boyfriend. I could tell you stories that would make you sick to your stomach, but all that shit don't matter no more. Deal with it and stop blaming others for why you out here acting a goddamn fool. A real man can be whatever he wants to be in life, and no bullshit from his past will stop him from making his dreams a reality. Start dreaming, muthafucka. If you really want to be a Street Soldier, step up your life. Take it to the next level; that way you don't have to resent men like me who figured out a way to the top. See you when you get there, if you got the balls to make it."

I got defensive because I didn't like his tone, nor did I appreciate what he was spilling to me. "Fool, I'm already at the top, thank you very much. And bein' a real man ain't all about havin' a lot of money. Get out of here with that shit."

"You damn right it ain't about money, but tell me this. How many kids do you have? Where are they right now?"

I cleared my clogged throat. Hadn't seen my son in a while and one other chick had recently confirmed that she had a daughter by me. I wasn't sure if I believed her or not. So many chicks were running around claiming that they had kids by me when, in reality, those kids belonged to someone else. "I got some kids. They with their mamas because I'm here."

"Yeah, I bet. You ain't at the top, fool. You're at the bottom of the barrel with the rest of those low-life assholes offering these young women out here nothing but a sick dick. You can't give nobody shit but sperm that does not pay bills. Then, you gripe about your father not being there for you, yet you abandon your own kids and put them in a position to turn out exactly like you. Man, wake the fuck up! Get your shit together and recognize the reality of your situation before it's too late."

Jaylin had pissed me off so badly that I jumped up to confront him. This nigga didn't know my struggle, yet he could stand there and judge me. His words had me shook up. Since I wasn't fucked up like I was yesterday, I was ready to deal with him. I touched his chest with mine, forcing him to back up.

"You ain't walked in my shoes, bruh, so don't stand there and pretend that you have. It's so easy for you to get at me like you are, but step out of the suburbs and bring yo ass down on Dr.

Martin Luther King, Union and Kingshighway to see how I get down. Get a feel for what my life is like every day and get to know my daily struggles. You don't have a clue, potnah, and see won't you get a cap popped in that ass for talkin'.yo shit."

Jaylin shook his head. He had a smirk on his face as he backed away from me. "Been there, done that. Lived on some of the same streets, but by choice, not anymore. I made a decision to trade in my shoes for comfortable ones that I could pay for with my own money. You're still wearing the ones that you done stole off another man's feet; that's why being in your shoes is difficult. You think that I'm supposed to fret when you jump up and threaten to hurt me? Fool, killing another black man only gets you classified as being stupid. I'm not afraid of you, Prince. A man who does not provide for his children, or who doesn't have the means to take care of self, does not move me. So, step the hell back before I crack you in your fucking face, again, and display my real North Kingshighway roots. You got until I count to three, and I'm already on two."

I seriously did not feel like going at it with this stuck-up asshole this morning. There was a time and place for everything, but this wasn't it. All I did was walk out, thinking about ways to make that nigga stay sleep for good.

Roc

Dinner was on the table. My intentions were to make sure it was better than breakfast. But as I looked at the table, I realized how badly the food was jacked up. The onion-filled hamburgers were almost as black as me and the fries were crisp and greasy. The only thing that wasn't burned was the cheese, and that was because I had slapped the slices on right before I put the burgers on the table. Everybody had a look of dissatisfaction on their faces, but there wasn't shit I could do.

"Eat up or be hungry," I said, giving options and scooting my chair up to the table. "I did the best I could do."

"It's just a burger, baby," Jada said. "Why did you have to be so mean to it? Once you saw it gettin' dark that should've been your cue to flip it."

"We forgive you," Chase said. "And I'm going to eat every single drop of this food on my plate."

"Bitch, ain't nothin' on your plate yet," Jada said. "So I guess you'll be eatin' nothin'."

"You don't know me like that to be callin' me no bitch, Jada, so chill out with that. And I am going to put some food on my plate, just not much."

While they were exchanging harsh words, Prince and Sylvia had gotten a few fries and one hamburger. I saw them picking around the edges, trying to remove the burnt pieces. I didn't expect for Jaylin to be sitting at the table, but he was. All he touched was his water and he winced at the burgers. It didn't matter to me if he ate or not, and on a for real tip, he could starve himself. He had nothing for breakfast, so I knew his stomach was fighting with him.

"You're not going to eat anything?" Sylvia said to him. I noticed the two of them getting kind of close, plus she had slept in the bed with him last night. Heard them talking and laughing, amongst a few other things that I suspected. I had plans to make some moves on Sylvia, to get underneath Jaylin's skin. I don't think there was ever a time when I had a beef like this with someone and didn't know how to handle it. I believed that Jeff would have me arrested for doing something to that fool, and I wasn't going back to jail over no bullshit. Jaylin wasn't worth all of that. Besides, Desa Rae would kill me. I couldn't even see myself being without her again, but it was hard for me to keep my anger in check.

After dinner, we did the usual. Some went outside to mess around, but I stayed inside to play Uno with Sylvia and Jada. Uno wasn't how I normally got down. I preferred craps, but since I wanted to see what was up with Sylvia, I decided to stay and make my move.

"I don't like playin' with y'all because y'all be cheatin'," I said, lying sideways on the living room floor. Sylvia was across from me, so I had an up-close-and-personal view.

"Jada is the one cheating," Sylvia snitched, laughing. "We busted her with two draw-four cards inside of her pants yesterday."

"You are so wrong for that," Jada said. "But today I have them hidden in my socks." Jada pulled several cards from her socks and laughed. "Now that I got busted again, I'm goin' outside to take a dip in the pool. I think the others are playin' volleyball, so Roc, I may need you to come outside to put a hurtin' on Jaylin. It's the only way I'll win."

"I'm comin'," I said, watching Jada get up. Sylvia did, too, but I touched her hand, asking her to chill with me for a while. "I haven't had a chance to holla at you and see what's up. I think we're the only two in here who ain't made no for real connection."

"You are so right," she said, sitting back down. "And if I'm going to win this challenge, I must get to know the people I'm competing with."

Jada threw her hand back and walked toward the door. "Hurry up, Roc. Don't leave me out here by myself, okay?"

"I promise. Ten minutes at the most."

Jada was gone, so Sylvia and I had a chance to chill. "What do you think of all of this so far?" I said. "Is it everything that you envisioned it would be?"

"And then some." She laughed. "I didn't realize how hard it would be for all of us to get along. I'm disappointed about what happened between you and Jaylin, and to be honest, I really don't trust the women around here. Jada and Chase are cool, but they're not the kind of women I normally hang around."

"I couldn't prevent the squabble that happened between Jaylin and me. He brought that shit to my doorstep, so I had to roll with it. I hated that it went down like that, especially in front of y'all."

"Are you still upset with him? I kind of felt as if all of this was my fault since I was the one who told him about Prince. For whatever reason, he thought you were in on it, but I reminded him that you had nothing to do with it or, at least, I hope you didn't."

"Nah, ma, I don't take anything from the next man. It's not my style. If Jaylin thought I took somethin' from him, he should've stepped to me like a man. He didn't, so we wound up lookin' like boys who weren't man enough to settle our differences."

"The two of you have had time to think about what happened and I hope it's behind you. I can't see things getting any worse than they've already been, or do you think I'm fooling myself?"

"From my point of view, I don't think they call this Hell House for nothin'. Prepare yourself because things will get much uglier."

I winked at Sylvia and left it there. Asked her to follow me outside, so we could join the others playing volleyball. I didn't care whose team I was on, as long as Jaylin was on the opposite team. I worked it to where me, Prince and Sylvia were on one team and Jada, Chase and Jaylin were on the other. Jada served the ball first and it went right into the net.

Jaylin sighed. "Are you telling me with those big, biscuit-looking arms you got that you can't even get the ball over the net? That's messed up, Jada, really it is."

"Fuck you, Jaylin. This ain't no damn Olympics where we can win a gold medal, so cool out with yo musty-dick self."

Jada had us cracking up and she didn't give a damn about what she said to anybody. The ball went to us, and Sylvia served it over the net. Chase hit it back over, and when I hit it, I tried my hardest to spike the ball at Jaylin's face. He dodged it by quickly moving his head.

"Watch yourself," he said to me. "Don't start none, won't be none."

I said nothing and pretended as if I didn't hear him. Sylvia served again, but this time the ball hit the net. "What you got to say about that, Jaylin?" Jada shouted. "Her arms ain't blowin' up like Pillsbury biscuits and she still didn't get the ball over the net either."

"I'd say the two of you need to sharpen your skills. Pay attention and learn something today."

At least an hour into the game, it had gotten ruthless. Nobody wanted to lose and we all were playing like there was a gold medal to be awarded at the end of the game. The score was 49 to

44 and the winner had to reach 50. My team was winning because Prince and I were determined not to lose.

"It's a done deal after this," I said, serving the ball to the other side. There was no doubt about it that the women were tired, but they kept on playing. They were soaking wet, especially Jada who swung at the ball, showing exhaustion and missed.

"Didn't you hear me say set it up?" Chase said with anger in her voice. "You're never going to get the ball over the net by swinging at it like you're hitting a baseball."

"That's what I'm talking about," Jaylin added. "What a way to lose the damn game."

On my side we were cheering. Just for the hell of it, I picked up Sylvia and proclaimed her the real winner. She was showing her pearly whites while being carried in my arms. More than that, she was happy to be on the winning team.

"Ugh," Jada said, getting out of the pool. She was so mad that she stomped into the house without saying a word. Jaylin and Chase wanted a rematch, but they weren't going to get it right now.

"How do you want me to repay you for workin' so hard?" I said to Sylvia, loud enough for Jaylin to hear.

"I don't know," she said. "What you got?"

"I can think of a million and one things, but you know I want you to be real satisfied, right?"

"I hope so because I worked my tail off so we could win this game. Somebody needs to give me something."

"Tonight, maybe I will."

The corner of my eye was in motion. Chase was hot, and even though Jaylin would never admit it, he was too. It was a double whammy for them both. I could sense hate a mile away, and I suspected all of it would be coming my way soon.

Chase

I had a problem and a serious one at that. There were two big-ass dicks in this house and neither one had been in me. Sylvia had been getting all of the attention and I didn't like it. First, she was all underneath Jaylin, and then her attention turned to Roc. She didn't appear to be playing by our rules, so I was going to pull her aside and have a little conversation with her, to see what was up.

Jada had been holding up her end of the bargain. I saw her flirting with Prince and hanging around him more often. He seemed to connect with her quite well. Then, why wouldn't he? They both were ghetto fabulous and the slang he used was terrible. Sometimes, I didn't understand a word he was saying and all that hip talk was driving me crazy.

Roc was guilty of using slang, too, and what in the hell was a "Ma?" I didn't mind his slang because his sexiness and the size of his penis made up for it. I swear that thing was huge, and when I sat on top of it in the bedroom that day, I could only imagine what it would feel like inside of me. We were almost there, but from what I knew now, he wasn't on the same page as me. It was unfortunate that he underestimated me as well; there wasn't a man on this earth that I wanted and couldn't get. Sure, some played harder to get than others, but when all was said and done, I was sure of a few things: I would have me a piece of the Roc,

Jaylin would be craving for more of me and the $100,000 that I needed so badly would be placed in my hands. Anyone who didn't believe me may want to put some money on it.

All day yesterday, and this morning as well, Roc had been on Sylvia like flies on shit. When she moved, he moved. Last night, they stayed up talking and didn't hit the sack until way after one o'clock in the morning. Roc had even gotten up to make breakfast for everyone. This time, it was a little better, and he prepared Sylvia's plate for her. He claimed it was for all the hard work she'd done while playing volleyball. But how much gratitude did he have to show her?

Yes, I was upset, only because he pretended to be down with me. I thought that after I told Sylvia and Jada what the men had been up to, we would all stick together and try to boot them out. But that wasn't happening. Sylvia was up to something and she needed to tell me exactly what it was.

With that in mind, after breakfast, I pulled her aside while she was on the computer.

"Hold up a minute, Chase," she said with a finger in the air. "Let me finish this real quick."

She was playing solitaire on the computer, and once she was finished, she met up with me in the hallway near the bathroom.

"Uh, what are you doing?" I said with my arms folded in front of me.

She played clueless. "What do you mean?"

"What I mean is, what's up with you and Roc? Or, should I be asking what's really up with you and Jaylin? You can't seem to make up your mind about who you really want to *screw* over, can you?"

Prince came out of the bathroom, bringing the smell of marijuana with him. I got sick of going into the bathroom smelling it, but I wasn't sure if it was him, Roc or Jada who had been firing it up. The mind was a terrible thing to waste and they were definitely wasting it.

"My bad," he said with red eyes and giggling. "Did I interrupt somethin'?"

"No," I said in a hurry, trying to get rid of him so Sylvia and I could finish our conversation. "We were just talking, that's all."

"Sounded more like yellin' to me. What y'all beefin' about now?"

"Nothing," Sylvia said, obviously irritated by him, too. "Nothing we won't be able to resolve."

"That's good news and the more peace we have in this house, the better. I'd hate to see the two of you bumpin' fists like Roc and Jaylin did, or like me and Jaylin did, 'cause that shit ain't cool."

"No, it wasn't. But do you think you can go find Jada or something, Prince? She was looking for you a little while ago. Said she had something important to give you."

"Straight? I've been lookin' for her," he slurred. "She good peeps and I'm down with any woman who can cook like she do."

I kept my mouth shut, realizing that as long as I kept talking, so would he. Sylvia didn't say anything else either until he walked away. She pulled her braids over to one shoulder and caught an attitude with me. "Just so you know, Chase, I'm not trying to screw either of them over. I want no part of your games; my gut tells me that you're the last person I should be trusting in this house."

My eyes bugged; I was surprised to hear her breaking news. I hated a two-faced bitch who could change her mind with the snap of a finger. She didn't want anything to do with our plan anymore because she felt as if dick was within her reach. I was so mad at this heifer that I let her have it. "So, let me get this straight. You don't trust me, but you trust Jaylin and Roc? Are you a fool or a damn fool? Which one?"

"You decide, but FYI, I don't trust anybody. Upset with me or not, I'm done playing games around here. It's too much confusion going on. If I'm going to win this challenge, I'm going to win by doing things my way, not yours."

"How are you doing it my way when you and Jada were the ones who gave suggestions about what we needed to do? Now all of a sudden you're singing a new tune. I wonder why that is, Sylvia? Because Roc is whispering all that sweet talk in your ear now, or because you're sleeping in the bed with Jaylin, fondling him at night? Women like you make me so sick, and no wonder the men viewed you as being the weakest link. They're still play-ing you. You're so caught up, not realizing what's real and what's not. My suggestion to you: get yourself together, bitch, before you get tossed out of this house on your ass with severely hurt feelings."

I was completely stunned when Sylvia stepped forward and smacked the shit out of me. My head snapped to the side and my cheek burned like fire. She smacked me so hard, my brain felt rattled. As many confrontations that I'd had with women, never had any of them put their hands on me like Sylvia had just done. I didn't have time to rub my cheek or cool it down; I had Sylvia pinned against the wall with my elbow shoved into her throat. She was taller than I was, but I applied enough pressure to her neck to keep her still.

"You fake tramp," I said through gritted teeth. "Don't you ever touch me like that again! I swear to God that if you do, I will set your whorish ass on fire while you sleep. If you don't believe me, feel free to try me again. All I tried to do was come to you woman to woman, but I see now what the hell I'm dealing with. A snake bitch who would rather have a piece of dick in her than walk away with respect and money."

I shoved Sylvia and she grabbed her throat, coughing and trying to catch her breath. Jada happened to see us and she rushed down the hallway to find out what was going on.

"What happened?" Jada said, looking at Sylvia who still couldn't get it together and catch her breath. She was bent over, trying to soothe her throat. Jada started patting her back real hard, fearing that she was choking. "Do you need some water?"

Sylvia moved her head from side to side, implying no.

"What she needs is a backbone," I said. "That trick slapped me, and I had to put her in her place. After telling her what the men were up to, Sylvia decided that she didn't want to be down with our plans. That's why she's been sucking up to Jaylin and Roc, saying to hell with us altogether. There is no telling what she has told them about us, so I suggest switching to Plan B, whatever that may be."

Jada backed away from Sylvia and gave me a mean mug. "No Plan B for me, and I am so done with you fake hoes. I swear a bunch of women ain't nothing but trouble, and you can count me out of the plan, too. I'mma do my own thing, so I'll see y'all at the finish line, if or whenever either of y'all get there. Good luck!"

Jada walked away, and after I rolled my eyes at Sylvia again, so did I. I was so mad because I don't care what it involved, some women just didn't know how to stick together. I couldn't wait until Sylvia got her walking papers out of here, and this was a prime example why I could not trust some women to follow through on anything.

I went into the bedroom and checked my face in the mirror. I had to be sure that that heifer didn't leave any marks on my face from that slap; it was pretty darn hard. I didn't see anything, but the slap made me think about the last woman who had put her hands on me. It was my boss, Liz, who had found out that her husband was in their bed with me, sucking me dry. Actually, I had been screwing him for days, in their bedroom, while she was supposed to be away on a business trip. So much for that, and when the smell of fire filled my nostrils, I jetted out of their burning house to save myself.

Liz's husband, Steven, rushed out of the house behind me to make sure I was okay. We could hear the fire trucks coming and neither of us could stop coughing. With his house up in flames, he was in a panic and told me to hurry up and vacate his premises so the neighbors wouldn't see me. I didn't even get a goodbye kiss, but while dressed in his robe, I hurried down the street to my car that had been parked in the same spot for several nights. Something didn't feel right to me, and I felt like someone was watching me. I thought hard about who could have done something like this, and since I had set my ex-boyfriend's house on fire, I thought it was him seeking revenge. Then again, I had so many enemies. Plenty of women were after me for having sex with their significant others, so there was no telling who was gutsy enough to pull something like this off.

Either way, I got in the car and jumped out of my skin when someone yanked the back of my ponytail. I couldn't see who it was in the rearview mirror because they had turned it in another direction. All I knew was that my neck was starting to hurt, and whoever had a grip on my hair was one strong motherfucker. I tried to move my head, but that was when I felt a sharp blade poke me in the face.

"One more move and I will slice you like bread," the woman said. I immediately recognized Liz's voice. "Don't you know that I've known about you fucking my husband for months? Do you think I'm that stupid? I know for a fact that the dick couldn't have been that good, where you had to run to my bed and get it. Bitch, are you crazy?"

She yanked my hair again, and I felt so helpless. Normally, I would be the one in control, but I had to cooperate with Liz or I was positive that she would kill me. She continued to remind me that her husband was off limits, and when her phone rang, she told me not to say a word or else. Her whole demeanor changed, and she listened to Steven tell her that their house was on fire, even though she was the one who had done it.

"Jesus, nooo. Honey, I can't believe our house caught on fire. The most important thing is that you're safe and I promise you that I will be home soon. I love you so much and we can replace every single thing inside of that house. I'm just glad that it wasn't worse."

Liz had the nerve to cry as she spoke. I had truly underestimated her, and Steven didn't realize the he had a real psycho bitch on his hands. I was glad that he'd gotten caught up, and it wasn't my house that burned, so I didn't really trip. I just wanted to make it out of this situation alive, but after Liz ended her call with him, she focused her attention back on me.

"You're lucky that I'm going to allow you to live, but my main focus right now is making that sleazy-ass husband of mine pay for sleeping with a tramp like you. If you ever come near us again, though, I will cut you up into a thousand pieces and bury you myself."

I knew Liz meant business. She shoved my head forward and hurried out of the back seat of my car. It wasn't long before I started the engine and took off, smiling. Why? Because I always admired a woman with balls, and one who knew how to get her husband where it hurt. There was a price to pay for being unfaithful. I hoped Steven would be able to deal with the consequences.

After that incident, I was done with Steven and with his crazy wife, Liz. She hadn't been on the up-and-up with him either, and what I later found out about her was devastating. So devastating that I wound up screwing her husband again, just because I felt like it. She never confronted me again, but if she did, I would be ready, just like I was when it came to dealing with Sylvia. Jada's fake self, too. I had my hands full with them, as I did with the men who I had major plans for.

After almost three weeks in this house, things had gotten real messy. Sylvia and Chase were still at each other's throats and they weren't speaking to each other at all. Roc and I continued on bad terms and Jada and Prince were the only two getting along. Or, at least, that was what I thought until last night. He playfully presented her with a dictionary and all hell broke loose. They started arguing and their argument turned into a food fight that had the whole damn kitchen in a mess. I was on the schedule to clean the kitchen, but they had me fucked up if they thought I was going to tackle the kitchen by myself. I didn't want to tackle it at all, but I had to play by rules.

The whole house needed to be cleaned and there was a lot of slacking going on. Never had I been in a house with piled up dishes, footprints on the floor, water stains on the shower and a toilet I refused to sit my ass on. I was the only one who made my bed every morning and the closet was starting to get messy, too. I expected this kind of lazy behavior from men, but the women knew better. Jada was too busy running her loud mouth all the time, Chase was too busy trying to plan her next move, and, Sylvia, I didn't know what the fuck she was doing.

Our conversation the other day led me to believe that everything was good with us. Then, she started playing these games with Roc to see if I'd get jealous. He was in on the shit, too, but didn't he know that I didn't give a fuck about Sylvia? He'd really been trying to get it in by cooking for her and rubbing her feet. I guess the fool was going to be polishing her toes next, and poor Chase was pissed off. All I did was laugh underneath my breath because the whole damn thing was silly. Silly as hell, but I for sure was no quitter. I was good at ignoring people and eliminating them from my mind as if they didn't exist. It was how I operated in the beginning, and it didn't take me long to get back to it.

"Jaylin, pass me the salt," Prince said while we sat at the kitchen table. I looked at the salt, but ignored him. Eventually, Roc passed it to him.

"Are you tense, sweetie?" Jada said, trying to tease me while we sat on the couch, watching TV. "I'll rub your back for you." I gave her a look that said what my mouth didn't open to say. And that was, keep your filthy, greasy hands to yourself.

"Jaylin, would you like some company when you work out in the morning?" Sylvia said. I didn't answer, but when she came into the workout room, I walked out.

"I sure do wish this house had a big-ole bathtub so I could fill it with bubbles and relax," Chase said. "Don't you, Jaylin?" No answer because if she had one, she wouldn't know how to clean it.

The only person who hadn't said anything to me at all was Roc. That all changed when I had come inside from swimming a few laps in the pool. I had wiped my face with a towel and he was standing near the bathroom.

"Brace yourself. I wouldn't go in there if I were you," he said.

"Why not?"

"One word. Prince."

"He straight up needs to go get his system checked out. My head start spinning every time I have to go into the bathroom after him."

"Well, it's a good thing that the rest of the house is clean. The bathroom? Not so much, but Chase will be gettin' down on that tomorrow."

"Clean? Is this what you consider clean? Nah, this house ain't clean by any stretch of your imagination."

"It's clean to me, but understand that we see things from a different perspective. Like we did when we got at each other. I'm not the kind of man who makes peace with everybody, but Prince broke everything down for me the other day. I guess I would've reacted the same way, if I thought somebody was tryin' to take from me, too. Where you tripped and bumped your head was when you put me dead smack in the middle of yo beef with Prince. Maybe your head wasn't on straight that day, but it happens to the best of us sometimes. So I say let's pack up this anger and place it elsewhere. Are you down with that 'cause the sisters are gainin' on us and we got a challenge to win?"

"Black man to black man, I guess we good." I held out my hand and he slapped his against mine. "I didn't have no beef with you, Roc, and I'm glad you understand where my anger was coming from. Prince tripped. I don't have much respect for that young man."

"I feel you, but like they say, if you want respect, you gotta earn it. Maybe he'll put forth some effort to get you to change your mind about him."

"I'm not going to hold my breath."

I did, however, hold my breath when I went into the bathroom to wash up. Before going to the bedroom, I emailed Jeff, requesting that he send a maid service in here to clean up. Unfortunately, I wasn't allowed to check my emails or visit any social networking sites. They'd all been blocked. I was surely wondering what my family, especially my kids, had been up to.

The day moved by pretty quickly, but at almost four in the morning, I found myself jumping in and out of sleep. I saw Sylvia tiptoe by my bed and make her way into the closet. I wondered what she was doing because it took a minute for the light to come on. Actually, it wasn't the light from the closet. It was a flashlight that I could see moving around. My eye twitched a bit; I became suspicious and I didn't trust anybody. As far as I was concerned, they were all conspiring against me. I had already taken my safe out of the closet, but my other items were still considered valuable. I had to go see what was up, so I could bust her in the act and possibly send her packing.

When I opened the door, I saw her sneaking to put something behind her back. She turned off the flashlight, but I flicked on the light switch.

"Up it," I said, holding out my hand. "What are you hiding?"

"Nothing. I was looking for something."

"Sylvia, you put something behind your back. All I'm saying is, I hope it doesn't belong to me or to anyone else in this house."

"I wouldn't take anything that belongs to someone else."

"Then show me what you got then."

She hesitated then slowly pulled her hand from behind and held out her clenched fist. When she opened it, inside was a torn picture. I looked at it, seeing that it was a picture of her and Jonathan.

"I keep dreaming about us," she said softly. "I want to move on so badly, Jaylin, but the relationship I had with him still haunts me. Only because I knew I was wrong for loving my best friend's man. I allowed myself to fall in love with him and I regret it. I regret that after all of this time, I still don't want to let him go. How can I make this stop? I need somebody to show me or tell me what must I do to free him."

A tear slipped from Sylvia's beautiful big eyes. I seriously felt her pain, even though it was sometimes hard for me to sympathize with women in her situation. Jonathan told me all about their relationship and I knew she had been in a bad position. I removed the torn picture from her hand and pulled her close to my chest, holding her.

"Stop torturing yourself and wanting to go back to the past. If it wasn't for you then, it won't be for you now. Let this thing with Jonathan serve as a big lesson learned and make room for a new man out there who may be dying for the opportunity to come into your life. He'll never find his way, if you continue to block his path."

Sylvia wiped her tear and backed away from our embrace. "I'm not trying to block his path. I just wish he would step forth so I can see him."

"Be careful what you wish for. I can tell you one thing, though. His name ain't Roc, so you need to stop playing these jealousy games with him."

"I'm not playing any games with him. But if it's not Roc, then who is it?"

"It ain't me either." I grinned, but was serious. "I can promise you that."

Sylvia finally smiled. "I'll take your word for it. I...I just don't know why I still have all of this anger inside of me, especially for Jonathan. Now that he's getting married, I feel dissed."

I folded my arms in front of me and rubbed my chin. "Dissed? Well, maybe you need to let out your frustrations. If Jonathan was standing here right now, in my place, what would you do?"

Sylvia narrowed her eyes and slapped me with as much force as she could. My head jerked to the side, and I wiggled my stinging jaw to ease the pain from the mediocre blow. I tilted my head, giving her an intense stare. "You may have to come better than that," I said. "What else would you do?"

Her eyes watered some more and then she tore into my bare chest with her fists. She pounded hard, but I barely moved. That was until she slapped me again, and I felt her sharp nail shave my cheek. I grabbed her wrist, twisting her arm behind her back and pushing her toward the wall so she could face it.

I moved in close and whispered near her ear. "If you got that much anger inside of you, use it wisely. Don't fight me, baby, fuck me."

I let go of Sylvia's arm and backed away from her. She turned around, keeping her eyes glued to mine as she placed her hand on the string to my silk pajama pants that hung low on my waist. She hit the light switch and got on her knees, facing me. My pajama pants were lowered to my ankles and she touched my growing steel with her hand.

"I'm not sure if I can handle all of this," she said. "But I'm sure as hell going to try."

"My wish is that you succeed. Get busy."

Her warm mouth covered most of my shaft that eventually expanded to reach the depths of her throat. With her mouth and swift hands in action, I closed my eyes and licked around my lips to catch my saliva. My weakening legs couldn't sustain the intensity of her dick sucking, and it wasn't long before I found myself caught in a situation where I couldn't regroup.

"That's right, baby," I said through deep breaths. "Get mad. Stay mad at that muthafucka for as long as you want to."

Sylvia was breaking a brother off with some mad head game. My dick was getting heavy in her mouth, and I could feel it pulsating. "I don't want to come like this." I backed away from her heat. "Take your pajamas off. Panties, too."

While Sylvia removed her pajamas, I sucked in heaps of air to regroup. My dick was sensitive to its touch. I definitely needed for it to calm down. It was all in the mind, so I cleared my thoughts of making Sylvia pay for slapping me, then I turned on the lights to look for a condom in one of my pockets. Sylvia lay back on the cushiony carpet with her perky breasts sitting at attention. I positioned my nakedness in between her wide legs, and took a glimpse of the sweet pussy I would add to my long roster of sexy women I had the pleasure of serving. I secured her lengthy legs around my waist, positioning my heavy meat to enter her.

"Are you sure you want this?" I whispered to her before going all in.

"Yes. All of it."

She was confident, and after three long strokes, her tunnel was filled to capacity. The tip of my head could go no further, and my balls smacked her ass with a kiss behind each hard thrust. I laid my pipe into her, bashing her goods and causing carpet burns to scold her ass. That was when she gasped out loudly and tried to tighten her legs. I rejected that move.

"No. Open. Wider," I commanded.

Sylvia stretched her legs, but the muscles in her pussy still had a strain on my dick. I could tell it had been a while since she'd had sex, but as her juices started flowing more, things loosened up for me. I put my hips in action, while she grabbed my ass and sank her nails into it. When I leaned forward, she sucked my lips into hers and tore my neck up with what felt like vampire bites. They were somewhat painful, but the feel of her coochie popping had my mind focused on where it needed to be. I painted every inch of her walls with my strokes and was ready to take this to the next level. After all, she was still mad, yet ready. I slowly pulled out, bringing down a flood of milky juices that dripped through the crack of her pretty ass. It was time to handle that ass, so I backed up a bit so she could roll on her stomach. She did, but also got on her elbows and knees, opening them wide enough so I could drive right in. But this time, I wanted to tease her. From the back, I slid my head through the edges of her long slit without entering her. The very tip of my head toyed with her hard pearl, along with the touch of my cold fingers. I kept sliding myself back and forth until she laced my whole shaft with her wetness. By this time, Sylvia was losing her mind. She tightened her fist, pounding it on the floor like a gavel.

"Put it in," she cried out. "Slide it all the way in, pleeeease!"

"You ain't ready for this," I said, continuing to tease her. "I don't think you're mad enough yet."

Nearing an orgasm, she pounded her fist on the floor again. "Muthafucka, I am ready! Gimme all of that dick, now!"

I admired a woman who didn't mind asking for what she wanted, so I drove my dick into her pussy going full speed ahead. Sylvia had cut the fuck up, and it was a long while before I put my nine-plus in park. All she could say was "Damn, Jaylin. Daaaamn!" as she worked on orgasm number three.

"What's my name again?" I said. "I want to make sure that you hadn't mistaken me for anyone else."

"Jaaaaylin, you-sure-do-know-how-to-fuck-a-woman, Rogers," she screamed out as I brushed my fingers against her clit to calm it. Sylvia, however, was hyped. Obviously, I had knocked Jonathan from her thoughts. She sat on top of me while resting back on her hands. Unable to do much moving, I held her legs far apart like a V, watching her in motion. No doubt, she had skills. It took major strength to work her lower body to a rhythm that kept me tuned in. All I could do was gaze down at the insertions and appreciate this new pussy that fit me like a warm glove. I hadn't sucked another woman's goodness in a very long time, but this one looked good enough to eat. I dropped her legs and wiped across my mouth. But as I got ready to change positions, I felt my muscle pulsating. Sylvia must have felt it, too, because she put in more overtime to make me come. I was there with her every step of the way, and when she shouted, I also released a buildup of semen into the condom. Sylvia dropped back on the floor and let out several deep breaths. I let out several, too, having no regrets whatsoever for what I had just done. Fuck Jonathan. His ass didn't know what he was missing.

"That…that was the best sex ever," Sylvia said with a heaving chest.

I couldn't agree with her on that, but I had to give her credit for giving it her all. The pussy was finger-licking good, but like most, it was forgettable.

Jada

A deaf person could hear Jaylin and Sylvia fucking in the closet last night. And by the way she was carrying on you would've thought that he murdered her pussy. If that heifer moaned one more time, I was going to get up and go shove a dirty sock in her mouth. I couldn't help but to touch myself from listening to them, though. I wanted to open the door to get a bird's-eye view of what that man was putting inside of her. Then again, I already knew because I had seen it with my own eyes. Sylvia was so lucky, and after thinking about what Jaylin had put on her, I couldn't help but to think about the last time Kiley and me were together and what he had put on me. Big girls needed love, too, even though I wasn't getting the kind of love I needed in this house from the men. Before getting out of bed, I laid there in a daze while staring at the bumpy ceiling and thinking about the only man who knew how to please me.

Kiley was so upset with me that day. He had just pistol-whipped my husband, Dwayne, for putting his hands on me during breakfast at IHOP. Kiley had saved the day, and I was doing my best to win him back, even though he'd fallen in love with a trick named Anna. The best thing about Kiley was that he would fuck my brains out whenever he was mad at me. That day was no exception, but when he pulled into the parking lot at the Hampton Inn, and we went inside to get a room, he tried to play like I meant nothing to him.

"*Why don't you stop playin' and just chill?*" *I said.* "*I don't know why you're upset with me and you're the one who left Dwayne for dead, not me.*"

"*I'm not playin', Jada! My damn pressure is up because of yo bullshit, and I'm not goin' back to jail for nobody!*"

"*I said I'm sorry. You don't have to keep yellin' at me, and I'm the last person who wants you to go back to jail.*"

Near tears because I was so sick and tired of arguing with this man, I got up to look in the mirror. I could see Kiley coming up from behind me, but when I opened my mouth to speak, he got angry.

"*Didn't I tell you not to say another goddamn word to me?*" *he yelled and yanked my pants and silk panties down to my ankles. I stepped out of them, and knowing what was in store for me, I pulled my shirt over my head. Minutes later, I stood naked, and once Kiley's shirt was off, he backed me up to the wall and squeezed on my right, healthy breast so hard that it hurt. I didn't say a word, because he reversed hurt with pleasure. His mouth covered my breast and his tongue went to work on my nipple, circling it. I was so hot and bothered that I lowered my hands to unbutton and unzip his sagging jeans. They were barely hanging onto his ass, so I reached my hand down inside of them, just to get a feel of his tight, muscular ass that was smooth, but solid as a rock like his chest was. He lifted one of my legs, securing it with his strong arm. While still against the wall, he then lifted me up so high that my pussy met up with his face. My thighs were balanced on his shoulders, and being in this position plenty of times before, I felt safe and secured.*

"*Suck me good, Kiley,*" *I ordered while preparing myself for what was next to come. His tongue dipped far into me and his entire mouth covered my hole as he sucked it. I immediately curled my toes to try and shake the intense feeling his fierce tongue delivered. I also rubbed his baldhead and cried out for him to give me more.*

"*Get it, baby. Get it good and don't let me down until my cherry burst into yo mouth.*"

Kiley barely responded to my dirty talk, but he damn sure appreciated it. "You are so fuckin' fine when you're angry like this," I said. "You be tearin' this pussy up! Hurry up and do your thing, so you can put that big dick inside of me."

I didn't care that Kiley had always been rough with me, and after I squirted his mouth with my excitement, he directed his pipe into me and kept his rhythm at a mediocre pace. It wasn't long before his pace increased and that was when he took a big girl like me into his arms and moved me inches away from the wall. While holding me up, he slapped his sweaty, naked body against mine and fucked me like it was going out of style. I could barely hang on and my body weakened with each hard thrust. My insides felt overly satisfied, and all I could do was throw my arms around his neck and tighten them. I begged for his love, and for our relationship that felt destined at times, yet so traumatic at others.

"I love you so much, boo. Just tell me what I need to do to get you to come back to me. You do still love me, don't you? Just…just tell me you still love me and that we still got a chance to be together. You know that bitch Anna can't please you like I can. Come home where you belong."

The more I talked, the harder Kiley worked. It seemed as if his dick grew bigger inside of me, and I was so ready to put in overtime and show this man how much I really loved him. I lowered my legs, causing him to pull out of me. His steel was dripping wet with my heavy glaze, but I backed him up to the dresser and dropped to my knees. He aimed his dick at my mouth, and I opened wide to receive all that he was willing to give me. We worked perfect together. My mouth swallowed him like a deep, warm pussy, and it was only then that I could get Kiley to speak.

"Yeah, ma, you are so good at that shit! Work that shit, girl, and swallow that muthafucka real good."

You'd better believe I did, and as he pulled at my hair, yanking it at times, I brought Kiley to his knees. He confessed his love for me that day, but less than two days later he was back with Anna. I told her what had happened between us. Kiley was so upset with me that he never reached out to me again.

Still thinking about how our relationship went down, a tear slipped from the corner of my eye. I wiped it away, only because crying over Kiley just wasn't worth it anymore. Memories were all I'd had, and after the ups and many downs in our relationship, I was perfectly fine with where things stood.

Wondering where everybody else was, I got out of bed and went into the kitchen. As expected, Chase was walking around with an attitude because Jaylin had given Sylvia some of his good stuff. It was her turn to cook breakfast, and I'll be damned if she didn't put a single grape on a plate with two slices of an apple next to it.

"Is this all we're supposed to eat?" I said, looking down at the plate as I held it in my hands.

"I don't feel like cooking anything. Besides, you could stand to lose some weight. No offense, Jada, so back off this morning, okay?"

How was I not to take offense to what she'd said? I didn't even feel like arguing with her this morning—had other stuff on my mind. She was already torn up because Jaylin still hadn't paid her no attention. He hadn't said much to Sylvia either, and after showering, he came into the kitchen, grabbed an apple and the newspaper and then whistled as he headed outside. For some reason, seeing his reaction put me in a better mood.

"Damn, you around here limpin' and shit this mornin' and he didn't even speak," I said, looking at Sylvia. "You would think that after all of the ruckus we heard last night, he'd be out here askin' you to marry him."

She threw her hand back at me, knowing damn well that her feelings were hurt. She had that zombie look in her eyes, and I don't know why she decided to go there with him.

"Marry me?" Sylvia said. "I don't think so, Jada. It's not at all that serious."

Chase had to add her two cents. "You can be sure that it's not, and I hope you'll be able to pick up the pieces, once all of this is over."

"Trust me, I will," Sylvia said, releasing a deep breath. "Now, if the two of you don't mind, I really don't wish to talk about what happened between Jaylin and me last night."

"That's fine with me," I said. "There's nothin' to talk about because we heard much of it. Just tell me this. Can you walk and was it really that good? I lost count after you came three times."

Sylvia corrected me. "It was more like four or five times, and I'll say that I'm not good at faking it. I didn't have to."

I couldn't do nothing but Dougie and high-five the nasty, trifling, stank-bitch for having that kind of sex with a man she barely knew. She had ventured and dared to go where Chase couldn't even get to. It was funny to me. Jealousy was so thick in Chase's eyes that she couldn't even roll the jealousy away.

"I guess we're not going to get anything else to eat, right?" I said to Chase.

"Nope." She headed toward the sliding doors. "I'm goin' to work out with Roc this morning. Maybe you should, too."

Oh, yeah, Roc. I had been giving Jaylin so much attention that I'd forgotten about Roc. The goal was to have both of them wrapped around my finger, so I followed Chase outside, while Sylvia headed to the bedroom.

As soon as I stepped on the patio, I saw Jaylin chilling back and reading the newspaper. Chase pursed her lips and marched toward the workout room, avoiding him altogether. I couldn't help but mess with him. "Hey, Jaylin," I said from afar. "Do you got a license to carry that concealed weapon with you? You kilt a bitch last night, didn't you? You were like…get mad, bitch! Whack, whack and you beat the shit out of her with that dick. She damaged for life and she can barely walk this mornin'.'"

All his ole funny-acting self did was stare at me. His eyes shifted back to the newspaper and he turned the page without saying a word. Sylvia definitely hadn't handled her business because, had it been me in that closet with him, he'd be running around here with pep in his step and acting like a fat kid about to get some cake.

Saying nothing else to Jaylin, I put up my middle finger, hoping that he wouldn't ignore that and shove it. I moseyed off into the workout room, where Chase and Roc were running side by side on treadmills. Prince was lifting weights. He was cut in all the right places, but not like Roc was. Without a shirt on, he looked like a black stallion. His basketball shorts were barely hanging on his ass, and I wanted to be somewhere in the vicinity if they fell off.

"Good morning," I said, making my way onto the treadmill to the left of him.

"What up?" he said, looking at me, as I tried to figure out how to start the damn thing. "Hit the green, quick-start button, baby. Then increase your speed to about thirty or forty."

I thanked Roc for helping me. What a way to get a sister's morning going by calling me baby! I increased the speed and started to jog on the treadmill like he and Chase were. We all were hanging in there, looking good and sprinting together. Then all of a sudden, after three minutes, my legs clashed together and started to burn. My calves tightened and I could barely catch my breath. I didn't want to slow down, but I had to. But when I touched the down button, the damn thing sped up. My legs tangled and the treadmill sent my ass flying off of it. I went crashing down on the rolling belt that carried me to the end of the treadmill and dropped me to the floor. My blubber shook; I was so damn embarrassed. I pretended that I hurt myself and grabbed at my ankle.

Roc stopped his treadmill to come cater to me. Chase and Prince couldn't stop laughing.

"Whaaaaaaaaa," Prince whined like a baby. "Damn! That shit felt like an earthquake."

Chase covered her mouth, trying to hold back her giggles. I was too mortified to cuss those fools out. Roc had a smirk on his face, too, but he bent down next to me. "Damn, ma, what happened?"

I squeezed my ankle and even forced out a tear as if I were seriously injured. Chase and Prince ole silly selves left in a fit of laughter, shaking their heads.

"I think I twisted my ankle," I said.

Roc took a light squeeze on it. "Can you feel that?"

I nodded. Of course I could.

"Can you stand up?"

"I think so."

He put my arm around his shoulder, helping me peel myself from the floor. I limped on one leg while he held my waist, making sure I didn't fall.

"How does it feel?"

Referring to his dick, I didn't know yet, but I would one day find out. This was too much sexiness to ignore, but I had to get him on my team first. "It's okay, Roc. It hurts a little when I step on it, but I should be okay."

He removed his arm from around my waist, but I still pretended to be helpless. Moments later, he swooped me up in his arms, carrying me without a sweat.

"I'mma take you to the couch so you can elevate your feet. It doesn't look swollen, and maybe all you need is some pain killers."

To hell with the couch; take me to the bedroom. That would surely cure me, but for now, all I did was smile. Roc crossed me over the threshold of the doorway, making me feel as if it were our wedding day. I secured my arms around his neck with a big smile plastered on my face. When we entered the living room, Jaylin was sitting on the couch, along with Chase who, yet again, got ate the hell up.

Roc carefully sat me down and then went to the kitchen to get my aspirin. "Tylenol or Advil?" he said, searching the cabinets.

"Tylenol," I said and then rolled my eyes at Chase.

"What happened to you?" Jaylin asked. At least he cared. For now, I had him and Roc wrapped around my finger, and I loved every minute of it.

"I fell off the treadmill. I'll be okay, so no need to worry about me."

As soon as Roc gave me the Tylenol and a glass of water, we heard someone enter through the front door. To our surprise it was Jeff. He spoke to us, and then he found the others and asked them to gather around. I wondered what was going on because Jeff looked to have something heavy on his mind. Maybe there was no fucking allowed in this house and Jaylin and Sylvia were about to get booted out. The rules mentioned nothing about intimacy, though, so I really wasn't sure why he was here.

Either way, we all spread out on the couch to listen in. Jeff scratched his head and combed back his blonde hair with his fingers.

"The time has come for someone to be voted out of Hell House. There are six of you and all six of you will decide who that person will be."

We all looked at each other because, all along, we thought that you had to leave on your own free will. No one could be voted out of here and this really didn't make sense. I guess the same question was on everybody's mind, so we all spoke at once.

"What the fuck?" Roc said out loudly. "You didn't say all of that."

"I'm confused," Chase said. "Why vote?"

"Trickery," Prince said. "This shit happens all the time."

Jeff lifted his hands, gesturing to try and calm the noise. "O... okay, everybody, calm down. From the beginning, we told you all that there may be some twists and turns in this competition. This is one of them."

"Well, I hope you don't decide to do a twist when it comes to uppin' the money," I said. "If you do, be prepared for me to twist your fuckin' neck because I don't play when it comes to money."

Many of the others agreed.

"The money situation is good," Jeff said, clearing that up. "But in order for you all to dwindle down to one, we must do it this way. So, take a minute to think about who you all want voted out of here today."

"Today!" Sylvia shouted. "Why today? It would be nice if you could give us a little time to think about this."

"Unfortunately not. You must decide immediately, and one-by-one, I need each of you to go over to the computer and email the name of the person you want to leave. At five p.m., I will email you that person's profile and picture. Feel free to answer your fan mail before you leave, but after that, the person voted off must leave."

"This is terrible," I said. "I feel like I got to backstab somebody, and I don't like to get down like that."

Jaylin stood up. "It's the rules, baby. Learn to follow them."

Without hesitating, he walked over to the computer. Logged in and typed in somebody's name.

"Done," he said, looking at Jeff.

My mouth dropped open. "Damn, it was that easy for you?"

He responded with a shrug. Afterward, Chase ran her trifling self over to the computer, logged in and did the same. She swiped her hands together and had the nerve to say, "Good riddance."

Then Sylvia almost broke her neck, rushing to the computer to login. She typed in a name and then hit the backspace key to make a correction. "Oops, sorry," she said. She logged out and walked away from the computer.

"Y'all some cold muthafuckas," Roc said as he sat down at the desk. He pondered for a minute and then slowly typed in a name. He also shrugged and walked away.

Now, it was Prince's turn because I was still in shock that nobody here had given this much thought. Prince laughed when he typed in a name and then said, "Done deal. Be gone, *Biatch*!"

What the hell! Really? Like it or not, it was my turn. I sat at the computer desk, pursing my lips and patting my leg, thinking hard about who I wanted to go home. I didn't know whose name to type because I could think of at least one good reason why every person in this house should be sent packing. Some I could think of several reasons. Either way, the decision didn't come easy for me, even though I couldn't stop thinking about getting my hands on that money. Finally, I forced myself to type in the person's name. I backed away feeling awkward, but hoping that the person leaving today wouldn't be me.

"Thank you, everyone," Jeff said. "Enjoy the rest of your day and say your goodbyes to everyone, just in case."

No one said a word. The room fell silent and all we heard was Jeff shut the front door.

"Well," Jaylin said, standing up and stretching. "It was fun while it lasted."

Roc smiled and cocked his neck from side to side. "Yes, it was, but somebody must go. Too bad it won't be me."

Prince slapped his hand against Roc's. "I second that motion, my nigga. Won't be me either."

"What makes you all so sure?" Chase said, standing and awaiting an answer.

Roc's eyes shifted to Jaylin and his eyes shifted to Prince. Neither of them said anything else, leaving some of us on the edge of our seats for most of the day.

The men indulged themselves in a rough game of basketball. Shirts were off and all of their bodies were dripping with sweat. It was fun to watch as they trash-talked each other, and I couldn't tell you how many times somebody had hit the ground or stumbled from being pushed. Sylvia, Chase and me watched them while chilling by the poolside.

"Be real careful with him!" I yelled to Prince as he pushed Jaylin in the chest. "I don't want Jaylin to fall and bust his head, 'cause y'all know he the only real brains we got around here!"

Prince lifted his middle finger, telling me to stick it. When he missed his shot, I laughed, just to irritate him and distract his game.

I guess I should have voted for him to leave the house, but I had somebody else in mind. Somebody who I truly thought should go home because they worked my damn nerves. I tried not to think about who was leaving, so I reached for the tall Long Island Iced Tea in front of me and sipped. I had put all kinds of different drinks in my glass. Surely enough to last me from here to Long Island, New York. It was good, though, but when Sylvia reached over to remove the twisted orange from the rim of my glass, I smacked her hand.

"I asked if you wanted one, but you said no. Please don't touch my orange; I plan to eat that."

All Sylvia did was smile, and when we glanced at Chase, her lust-filled eyes were still glued to the men on the court. I swear I had never, ever been around thirsty-ass women like Chase and Sylvia. Now, I had some dick-happy friends, but these hoochies took the word *thirsty* and ran with it. Jaylin's and Roc's heads had probably swelled so big since they'd been here, and I wasn't talking about their lower heads that had gotten all of the attention. I had to blow my breath in Chase's face and call her name, twice, to get her attention. She blinked her eyes and was now back from her zombie-like status.

"Wha...what did you say?" she asked.

"I asked that you please clear your filthy, nasty, cluttered mind and stop droolin' from yo mouth. I can tell what you're thinkin' and it damn sure ain't about those cookies I baked earlier."

"Not hardly, but the cookies were good. Real good, just not as good as my thoughts. I hope that I'm here long enough to live out some of the little fantasies I have swirling around in my head."

"You may have to play out your fantasies elsewhere because there ain't no tellin' which one of us is goin' home. I hope and pray it ain't me because I sholl do need that money."

"I could use the money, too," Sylvia said. "But more than anything, it would be a true let down to be the first person voted out of the house. That would sting."

"Big time," Chase said. "And, Jada, since you're so sure about me not living out my fantasies, I take it that you voted for me, huh?"

"I'm not sayin' who I voted for, but whoever it was, I did so because that person was workin' my nerves. If you've been doin' it, then there is a possibility that I voted for you."

Chase threw her hand back and spoke the truth. "Everybody in this house has been working your nerves. So, I'm sure it was hard for you to vote."

I had to laugh because Chase was so right. Her eyes were now glued back on the men, as they headed our way. They came up to the table with heaving chests and a whole lot of loud mouthing.

"Y'all always cheatin'," Prince griped while standing next to

Chase. Roc was to my left and Jaylin was to my right, trying to explain to Prince why he kept losing.

Roc added his two-cents, too. "Your jump-shot is weak and you need to learn how to hold your hands when you take it."

Roc gave him an example, but Prince wasn't trying to hear him. He looked away, but all Roc did was shrug. He picked up my Long Island Iced Tea and, as he took a few swallows, I pulled on the rubber waistline of his basketball shorts to take a peek at his goods. He inched back and moved my hand.

"Boy, why you ain't got on no underwear? You don't have to answer, but ladies, I can tell y'all this." I looked at Chase and then Sylvia. "I did not vote for that man to leave the house. No siree."

They shook their heads and giggled. I turned to Jaylin and pulled on his shorts to take a peek, too.

"Lord knows I didn't vote for him either, and all of that must stay, too."

My eyes shifted to Prince, but he dared me to touch him. I didn't mention out loud if I voted him out of the house or not, because I wanted him to think that I did.

I faced Roc who was still killing my Long Island Iced Tea. "Who you vote for, Roc?"

"You."

I pointed to my chest, but could tell he was playing by the smirk on his face. Then again, I wasn't so sure. "Me? Why me?"

"Because you talk too much. Besides, it ain't really none of yo business who I voted for. You soon shall see."

I snatched my empty glass from his hand. "It may not be my business, but that drink was. Please go hook me up before I have to go in there and change my vote to you."

Roc removed the towel from around his neck and popped it against my leg. The pop hurt, and what he'd done sparked a playful fight between us. After I got done beating him up, I jumped on his back and he carried me into the game room to make another Long Island-Long Ocean Tea. While we were away from the others, I could see them from afar, chatting it up and laughing. There really wasn't a doggone thing funny, and when five o'clock rolled around, we all realized that this was no joking matter. Somebody was going home and none of us were ready to receive our walking papers.

We all surrounded the computer desk, gazing at the monitor with a twenty-five-inch screen. The room was so quiet that the only thing you could hear was the chatter of Chase's rotten teeth. My palms were sweating and my stomach tightened when the person's profile and picture came up on the screen. All eyes turned in the same direction, and all I could say to myself was *damn*. You ain't got to go, but it was time for whomever to get the hell out of here!

BOOK CLUB QUESTIONS

1. Who do you think will be voted out of *Hell House*? Why?

2. Who is your favorite person in the house and why?

3. Who is your least favorite person in the house and why?

4. Which person reminds you more of yourself and in what ways?

5. Would you ever move into a house with six other people to win $100,000?

6. Which Brenda Hampton novel are you more likely to read after your Hell House experience?

7. If you were in this house, would you be interested in having a sexual experience with Roc, Jaylin or Prince? Why?

8. The *Hell House* trilogy opens the door to reality TV book reading. Did you feel like you were watching reality TV, and what show did it remind you of, if any?

9. Create your own reality TV show. Who would you like to have inside of a house with you for three months?

10. Who do you ultimately think will win the *Hell House* challenge?

AUTHOR'S NOTE

I'm eager to hear from you! Please visit hellhouse.homestead. com to send comments regarding your *Hell House* experience. If you would like to ask questions or send "fan mail" to any of the characters, and possibly have your inquiry answered in the books following, please follow the submissions guidelines.

READING JUST GOT MORE FUN!
Naughty 1
Naughty 2
Naughty 3
Naughty 4: Naughty by Nature
Naughty 5: Too Naughty
Naughty No More
Jaylin's World: Dare to live in it!

Full Figured 1
Full Figured 3
Full Figured 5
Who Ya Wit (Full Figured Finale)

How Can I Be Down?
No Justice No Peace

Street Solider 1
Street Solider 2

In My Shoes: A Writer Is Born
SLICK
Don't Even Go There
Two Wrongs Don't Make a Right
The Dirty Truth
If Only for One Night
Don't Ask Don't Tell
Girls From Da Hood 5
No Turning Back

ABOUT THE AUTHOR

A St. Louis native, Brenda Hampton is recognized for being a writer who brings the heat. She has written over twenty-plus novels, including anthologies, and her literary career is filled with many accomplishments. Her name has graced the *Essence* magazine bestsellers list, and she was named a favorite female fiction writer in *Upscale* magazine. Her mystery novel, *The Dirty Truth*, was nominated for an African American Literary Award, and she was awarded, by Infini Promotions, for being the best female writer.

Hampton's dedication to her career, and her original literary works, led to a multibook deal. She works as a literary representative for an array of talented authors, and she is the executive producer of an upcoming reality TV show, based out of St. Louis, Missouri where she resides.

In an effort to show appreciation to her colleagues in literature, Hampton created The Brenda Hampton Honorary Literacy Award and Scholarship Fund. The award not only celebrates writers, but it also represents unique individuals who put forth every effort to uphold the standards of African-American literature. Visit the author at www.brendamhampton.com and www. hellhouse.homestead.com